Lernkrimi Business English

THE 25 MILLION COUP

Bernie Martin

Compact Verlag

Bisher sind in dieser Reihe erschienen:
- Englisch, Französisch, Italienisch, Spanisch: B1, B2
- Englisch GB/US, Business English: B1, B2
- Deutsch: B1
- Sammelband Lernkrimi Englisch, Spanisch: B1/B2

In der Reihe Compact Lernkrimi Kurzkrimis sind erschienen:
- Englisch, Französisch, Italienisch, Spanisch, Deutsch: A2

In der Reihe Compact Lernkrimi History sind erschienen:
- Englisch: B1, B2, Italienisch: B1

In der Reihe Compact Lernthriller sind erschienen:
- Englisch: B1, B2, Spanisch: B1

In der Reihe Compact Lernstory Mystery sind erschienen:
- Englisch: B1, B2

In der Reihe Compact Lernkrimi Hörbuch sind erschienen:
- Englisch: B1, B2, Business English: B2
- Französisch, Italienisch, Spanisch: B1

In der Reihe Compact Lernkrimi Audio-Learning sind erschienen:
- Englisch: A2, B1

In der Reihe Compact Lernkrimi Sprachkurs sind erschienen:
- Englisch: A1/A2

Lernziele:
- Grundwortschatz, Grammatik (A2, B1)
- Aufbauwortschatz, Konversation (B2)

In der Reihe Compact Schüler-Lernkrimi sind erschienen:
- Englisch, Französisch, Spanisch, Latein, Deutsch, Mathematik, Physik, Chemie

Weitere Titel sind in Vorbereitung.

Chefredaktion: Dr. Angela Sendlinger
Redaktion: Patrizia Ginocchio
Fachredaktion: Angela Billington
Produktion: Wolfram Friedrich
Titelillustration: Karl Knospe
Typographischer Entwurf: Maria Seidel
Umschlaggestaltung: Carsten Abelbeck

ISBN 978-3-8174-7659-6
7276593

Besuchen Sie uns im Internet: www.compactverlag.de, www.lernkrimi.de

Vorwort

Mit dem neuen, spannenden Compact Lernkrimi können Sie Ihre Englischkenntnisse auf schnelle und einfache Weise vertiefen, auffrischen und überprüfen.

Inspector Hudson erleichtert das Sprachtraining mit Action und Humor. Er und seine mysteriösen Kriminalfälle stehen im Mittelpunkt einer zusammenhängenden Story.

Der Krimi wird auf jeder Seite durch abwechslungsreiche und kurzweilige Übungen ergänzt, die das Lernen unterhaltsam und spannend machen.

Prüfen Sie Ihr Business English in Lückentexten, Zuordnungs- und Übersetzungsaufgaben, in Buchstabenspielen und Kreuzworträtseln!

Ob im Bus oder in der Bahn, im Wartezimmer, zu Hause oder in der Mittagspause – das Sprachtraining im handlichen Format bietet die ideale Trainingsmöglichkeit für zwischendurch.

Schreiben Sie die Lösungen einfach ins Buch!

Die richtigen Antworten sind in einem eigenen Lösungsteil zusammengefasst.

Und nun kann die Spannung beginnen ...

Viel Spaß und Erfolg!

Inhalt

Story

James Hudson arbeitet als Inspector bei der legendären Polizeibehörde Scotland Yard. Er ist einer der fähigsten Männer und wird immer dann zu Rate gezogen, wenn seine Kollegen mal wieder vor einem Rätsel stehen. Seine resolute und krimibegeisterte Haushälterin Miss Paddington unterstützt ihn stets mit liebevoller Fürsorge.

Skandal im Bankenviertel: Aus der renommierten Warminster Bank in der Londoner City verschwinden 25 Millionen Pfund – und der klügste Kopf unter den Anlageberatern. Hat sich Charlie Greaves mit den Millionen aus dem Staub gemacht?
Hudson und die reizende Elvira Elliot untersuchen den Fall vor Ort und stoßen dabei auf viele Fragen und einige Merkwürdigkeiten.
Wird es Inspector Hudson gelingen, Licht in die Angelegenheit zu bringen? Eines ist jedenfalls sicher: Erst wenn Hudson das Geheimnis um Charlies Verschwinden aufdeckt, kommt er auch den Millionen näher.

Chapter 1: A New Case for Hudson

Hugh Montgomery gave a sigh of frustration.

"Charlie," he said, "I'm sure that you'd lose your head, if it wasn't screwed on." Charlie Greaves paused in his search for the slip of paper that had his computer password written on it.

"It must be here somewhere. Ah! Here it is. It must have slipped under my diary, while I wasn't looking."

Scratching his head, Charlie started taking his coat off, knocking the stapler off his desk with his arm. Hugh grinned and rolled his eyes at their colleague, Jeremy Paxton.

"Why don't you change your stupid password to something that you can remember?" Paxton hissed, obviously annoyed.

Hugh threw a ball of paper at Paxton and said, "stop picking on Charlie, Jeremy. You know he works hard. He's a mathematical genius and we'd be lost without him."

Paxton stood up and started pulling files from the filing cabinet. "It's just so annoying. Every morning Charlie comes in and causes havoc, looking for things that a five-year-old wouldn't lose. In the last few weeks he's lost his hole punch, rubber, ruler, calculator, sellotape..."

"Okay, Jeremy, that's enough," Hugh said, his voice getting louder. "Why don't we just calm down and I'll get us some coffee. Jeremy?"

Paxton nodded sourly.

"Charlie?"

They both looked at Charlie who was muttering something about his glasses, completely unaware of his two colleagues.

Hugh did his best to keep his voice calm. "Charlie, your glasses are on your head. Now then, would you like a coffee?"

Charlie pushed his glasses onto his narrow nose with an embarrassed grin.

"Yes please, Hugh. Black with two sugars."
Hugh left the office shaking his head.

ÜBUNG 1

Übung 1: Unterstreichen Sie im vorangegangenen Textabschnitt die englische Entsprechung der Wörter in Klammern!
(1. Terminkalender, 2. Heftmaschine, 3. Aktenschrank, 4. Locher, 5. Radiergummi, 6. Lineal, 7. Taschenrechner, 8. Klebeband)

Hugh returned with three plastic beakers of coffee twenty minutes later.
"That took you long enough. Have you been flirting again?"
Ignoring him, Hugh put Charlie's coffee on his desk.
"Listen, Charlie. I've been thinking about what Jeremy said earlier. He's right, you know. You do need to change your password to something you can easily remember. If you did lose it, we'd have to call the IT department in and that would cause a lot of hassle."
"You're right, Hugh. But I have to go through these figures first. The deadline is a week tomorrow."
"No, Charlie. Do it now, otherwise you'll just forget again."
Charlie gazed up at the ceiling with a blank expression on his face. All of a sudden, he gave a huge smile, typed something into his computer and said, "Got it!"
"Good man, Charlie. Do you need any help with those figures?"
"No thanks, Hugh. Sir Bernard asked me to do an analysis of all our investments over the last two months. It's pretty complicated, but I'm confident that I'll have it finished by the deadline."
Frowning, Hugh returned to his desk. He couldn't help noticing that Jeremy Paxton had been listening very closely to their conversation. He glanced at him, but Paxton quickly looked away and pretended to be busy.

Übung 2: Welches Wort für „Null" passt in welchen Kontext? Setzen Sie ein!
(oh, zero, love, nought, nil)

1. football scores: nil
2. tennis scores: love
3. after a decimal point, telephone numbers, bus numbers, hotel room numbers and years: oh
4. before a decimal point: nought
5. for the number or temperatures: zero

Inspector James Hudson sat at his desk in his Scotland Yard office, trying to figure out his new mobile phone. His boss, Sir Reginald, had insisted that Hudson should be permanently contactable. Hudson, his face screwed up in concentration, was attempting to enter important phone numbers into the mobile's address book. He had to refer to the instruction manual frequently and he was having real problems referring to the manual, his own leather telephone book and the mobile's display simultaneously. Just as he thought that he was getting the hang of it, the normal telephone on his desk rang shrilly, causing him to drop the mobile phone. Cursing frustratedly, he picked up the receiver and barked,

"Yes?"

"Ah! Inspector Hudson. Sir Reginald speaking. Could you spare a few moments?"

"Of course, sir. Sorry if I was a little abrupt, but I've been trying to work out my new mobile phone."

"Wonderful, Inspector. My secretary also received one and she said that it's the most uncomplicated mobile phone she has ever used."

"Well, I'm very happy for her, sir. Should I pop along to your office right away?"
"Please do, Inspector. I'll have a nice cup of your favourite Earl Grey and some chocolate biscuits waiting for you."
Hudson stood up, looked down at his desk and shook his head in despair. He put on his jacket with a sigh of resignation and left his office muttering sarcastically. "The most uncomplicated mobile phone ..."

ÜBUNG 3 !

Übung 3: Übersetzen Sie!

1. Geben Sie mir bitte Ihre Handynummer!

Please give me your mobile number

2. Vergessen Sie nicht, die Vorwahl zu wählen.

Don't forget do the precall

3. Ich schicke Ihnen morgen eine SMS.

I send you ~~on~~ a SMS tomorrow

4. Der Akku muss alle paar Tage aufgeladen werden.

5. Ich kann im Keller kein starkes Empfangssignal bekommen.

Inspector Hudson was shown into Sir Reginald's office as soon as he arrived.
Sir Reginald barked in his bulldog voice, "Inspector Hudson, please take a seat. Tea?"

Hudson accepted with a nod and Sir Reginald instructed his secretary to bring tea and biscuits.
"Right, Inspector. I'm afraid we have a slight problem."
Hudson knew from experience that when Sir Reginald said 'we', he actually meant 'you'. In addition, a 'slight problem' normally meant a big one.
"What's the problem then, sir?"
"Have you heard of The Warminster Bank, Inspector?"
"Yes sir, I have. They have their headquarters in Threadneedle Street."
"Correct. Well, I received a phone call from Sir Bernard Patterson an hour ago. He's the bank's director in charge of investments, by the way."
"I see, sir," said Hudson. Although he didn't.
"Well, he told me that some money seems to have vanished from the bank."
"Was the bank broken into, Sir Reginald?"
"No. The 25 million seem to have been stolen electronically."
Hudson whistled softly.
"25 million pounds. That is a lot of money."
"It certainly is, Inspector, but that's not all."
"Do you mean there's more, Sir Reginald?"
"I'm afraid so, Inspector. Sir Bernard instructed his best expert, a Charlie Greaves, to analyse all the bank's transactions for the past two months. The report was due today, but nobody in the bank has seen Mr Greaves since yesterday. He seems to have vanished into thin air."
"Perhaps he's just sick, sir."
"He's not, Inspector. When he didn't show up for work this morning, Sir Bernard called his wife. She said that Greaves didn't come home from work yesterday, but she assumed that he was

working non-stop. Apparently he does that now and again."

"So we can surmise that Greaves has done a runner with the money and left his poor wife behind."

"Don't count your chickens before they're hatched, Inspector. Sir Bernard insists that he isn't the criminal type. Besides, a man is innocent until proven guilty, you know."

"Of course sir. Well, I'll get onto it right away. If you could give me Sir Bernard's telephone number, I'll arrange an appointment with him."

"My secretary will provide you with it on your way out, Inspector. Needless to say, this case should be handled with kid gloves. Oh, and no press. There are some very influential people on the board of the bank and I promised we would keep a low profile for the time being."

"Right, sir. My lips are sealed."

"Oh, Inspector. One last thing."

"Sir?"

"When you leave the building, don't forget to take your new mobile with you."

"Yes sir," Hudson said with a resigned sigh.

ÜBUNG 4 !

Übung 4: Bilden Sie aus den Wörtern sinnvolle Sätze!

1. seat please a take

Take a seat please

2. slight have I'm problem we afraid a

I'm afraid we have a slight problem

3. due today was the report

Due to the report today

4. an him I'll with arrange appointment

I'll arrange an appointment with him

5. show up work he morning didn't for this

6. right onto I'll it away get

right away I'll

Hudson collected the number from Sir Reginald's secretary and returned to his office. He immediately placed the call and was given an appointment for 2 pm. He glanced up at the clock and saw that it was nearly half past twelve. Normally, his housekeeper, Miss Paddington, had to remind him to eat, but his growling stomach informed him that he should eat lunch before leaving for the bank. He left his office in a hurry, hoping to avoid the twelve-thirty rush for the canteen.

The silence of his office was peaceful, like the calm before a storm. The faint ticking of the clock and hum of traffic in the distance were the only detectable sounds. Suddenly, the door flew open and a red-faced Inspector Hudson burst in, snatched the mobile phone from his desk and rushed out again mumbling something about, "Sir Reginald, blasted mobile, canteen, too late..."

Übung 5: Was bedeuten die englischen Redewendungen? Kreuzen Sie an!

ÜBUNG 5 !

1. Don't count your chickens before they're hatched.
   a) ☐ Don't treat something as a certainty.
   b) ☐ Don't count your money.

c) ☐ Expect something bad to happen.

2. the calm before the storm
   a) ☐ to be expecting good weather
   b) ☒ the peace before something exciting happens
   c) ☐ the signal to finish work

3. to be all ears
   a) ☐ to have very big ears
   b) ☒ to listen very carefully
   c) ☐ to listen at a keyhole

4. to speak one's mind
   a) ☒ to express your feelings openly
   b) ☐ to tell lies
   c) ☐ to say something undiplomatic

5. to meet someone halfway
   a) ☐ to meet someone in a neutral place
   b) ☐ to meet someone on the way to work
   c) ☒ to make a compromise with someone

Chapter 2: Hudson Begins his Investigation

Hudson arrived at the bank a few minutes before his appointment. It was obviously a very traditional bank with wood panelling on all the walls. Behind the mahogany reception desk was a picture of an old-fashioned gentleman dressed very conservatively and with huge side whiskers. The caption below the portrait read: Our founder, Lord Warminster. 1853.

Übung 6: Lesen Sie weiter und setzen Sie die Wörter in Klammern in die Lücken ein!
(this, for 2x, on, in, that)

The receptionist was busy (1.) on the telephone, but she smiled a welcome and motioned (2.) for him to take a seat.

"Yes, Lady Patterson. I'll remind Sir Bernard (3.) that you have dinner guests (4.) this evening and that he should leave work early. Thank you (5.) for calling. Goodbye Lady Patterson."

The receptionist replaced the receiver, made a note (6.) in her business diary and turned to Inspector Hudson smiling.

"Good afternoon, sir. Welcome to Warminster Bank. How can I be of assistance?"
"Good afternoon. My name's Inspector Hudson of Scotland Yard and I have a 2 o'clock appointment with Sir Bernard Patterson, Ms...?"
Pointing at the badge on the lapel of her blouse, the receptionist said, "my name's Martorelli, Inspector. Anna Martorelli. Sir Bernard's in a meeting, but I was instructed to inform him as soon as you arrived."
"Thank you, Ms Martorelli. I'll just wait here then, shall I?" Hudson asked politely.
"Please do. It shouldn't take too long. May I offer you something to drink while you're waiting?"
"No thanks. I'm fine."
Hudson settled down to wait, flipping through some financial brochures.

Übung 7: Wie würde man auf höfliche Art und Weise fragen? Kreuzen Sie die richtige Lösung an!

1. Sie stellen sich vor.
   - a) ☐ Hi, I'm Fred. Who are you?
   - b) ☐ It's me! Fred.
   - c) ☒ Hello. My name's Fred Winters.

2. Sie fragen jemandem nach seinem momentanen Befinden.
   - a) ☐ Hi! What's up?
   - b) ☐ How are you doing?
   - c) ☒ How do you do?

3. Sie fragen jemanden, ob er ablegen möchte.
   - a) ☐ Do you want to take your coat off?
   - b) ☒ Would you like me to take your coat?
   - c) ☐ Must I hang your coat up?

4. Sie bieten jemandem etwas zu trinken an.
   - a) ☒ May I offer you something to drink?
   - b) ☐ I suppose you want a drink?
   - c) ☐ Do you want some water?

Hudson heard Sir Bernard before he saw him.
"I'll get to the bottom of this, if it's the last thing I do."
Sir Bernard stormed into the reception area like a tornado, with a harried-looking woman carrying a notebook, trying her best to keep up with him. Hudson's trained eyes saw a very tall, skinny gentleman wearing a pin-striped suit.
"I wonder if he wears a bowler hat too," mused Hudson. "He certainly looks the part with his steel grey hair and aquiline nose."

He stood up and unconsciously straightened his tie.

"Ah! You must be the chap from Scotland Yard. Pleased to meet you, old boy."

With that, Sir Bernard grabbed Hudson's hand and shook it up and down energetically.

"He's probably been doing too much business with Europeans," Hudson thought.

"Pleased to meet you too, Sir Bernard. I'm Inspector James Hudson."

"Actually Inspector, we were just about to start an emergency meeting about the missing money and of course, Greaves. We will try to decide the right course of action."

"Well, Sir Bernard. I think it would be a good idea if both of us went to the meeting. It would give me the chance to observe the people involved."

Sir Bernard's eyes widened in shock.

"That's an unusual request, Inspector. However, I don't think it will be a problem. Follow me, Houston."

"Er, it's Hudson, sir."

"What? Of course. Follow me, Hudson."

Sir Bernard took off like a greyhound and Inspector Hudson, and of course the lady with the notebook, tried their best to keep up.

Übung 8: Welches Wort ist das „schwarze Schaf"? Unterstreichen Sie das nicht in die Reihe passende Wort!

1. follow, trail, catch, track
2. stapler, hole punch, lamp, ruler
3. observe, look, write, see
4. pounds, dollars, money, cents

5. tie, suit, shorts, jacket
6. computer, software, printer, modem

Hudson was just starting to get a stitch in his side, when Sir Bernard took a sharp left turn and threw open a heavy oak door. The chatter taking place in the room came to an abrupt halt and everybody stared at Hudson.

"Ladies and gentlemen," Sir Bernard announced, "let me introduce you to Inspector Hudson of Scotland Yard, who has come to assist us with our little problem. Inspector Hudson would just like to observe. Does anyone have a problem with that?"

Sir Bernard peered around the room, as if daring anybody to protest. There were no verbal objections, but some of the people's expressions certainly gave Hudson the impression that he wasn't welcome. As he took a seat, the people started whispering to each other. An elderly, distinguished looking gentleman sitting at the head of the conference table raised his voice.

"Order. Ladies and gentlemen. Order please."

Gradually things quietened down and when he was satisfied, the man continued.

"Please carry on taking the minutes Ms Baxter. Now then. Welcome Inspector. Let me introduce you to the members of the board, who are all present today. I am Lord Montgomery. I'm the Chairman of the board and I am chairing this meeting."

Hudson was duly impressed. Studying him more closely, Hudson noticed that the Earl's hands were trembling slightly. He took out his notebook and started noting things down.

"To my left is my dear wife, Lady Montgomery, who in fact owns fifty-one per cent of the shares."

Hudson wrote: *Very aristocratic, also well-groomed. Eyes of steel!*

"To my wife's left is my lovely daughter Penelope."

Penelope Montgomery stared bitterly at Hudson. He tried to break her stare, but was unsuccessful. He noted: *If looks could kill, I would now be dead!*

“Sitting next to me on my right is Nigel Broadhurst, a very successful entrepreneur from Yorkshire.”

Broadhurst, who was rather obese, gave Hudson a nod and a wink from one of his twinkling eyes.

“And last, but not least, to your right is Dame Ethel Trowbridge.”

Hudson turned to his right to greet the lady, but she seemed to be fast asleep.

“Dame Ethel. I say, Dame Ethel!”

The quaint old lady woke with a start and asked in a high-pitched tone, “Is it time for tea and biscuits?”

Hudson hid a smile behind his hand and the meeting continued.

Übung 9: Übersetzen Sie und enträtseln Sie das Lösungswort!

ÜBUNG 9

1. Protokoll minutes
2. teilnehmen attend
3. abstimmen vote
4. vorstellen introduce
5. Vorsitzender chairman
6. Leistung performance
7. Ziel goal

Lösung: Meeting

“Right. Sir Bernard. Would you be so kind as to give us a run-down of the events that have led to this emergency meeting?”

“Certainly, old chap. My pleasure. Well, a few months ago, I re-

ceived reports of money going missing. At first it was just a few thousand pounds here and there. I figured that they were possibly due to miscalculations, which has happened in the past. But suddenly, a few days ago, huge amounts were disappearing. The total amount currently is about 25 million pounds!"
Penelope Montgomery shouted above the murmurs.
"I don't believe what I'm hearing. Are you trying to tell me that somebody withdrew 25 million pounds out of our accounts and we don't know who, or even how?"
Sir Bernard went red in the face and blustered. "All our IT department can tell me at the moment is that the transactions were made from a computer within our bank. I hate to say this, ladies and gentlemen, but it appears to be an inside job."

! ÜBUNG 10

Übung 10: Welches Wort gehört in die Lücke? Lesen Sie weiter und setzen Sie ein!
(arrogantly, capable, assured, cooperate, somebody, employees)

Mr Broadhurst, wiping sweat from his brow, looked as though he was about to have a fit. "Are you saying, that one of our (1.) ________________ has stolen all this money, Sir Bernard?"
"I'm afraid so. It must be (2.) ___________ who works in the bank."
"Well, I for one would like to know what you are doing about it," demanded Lady Montgomery very (3.) ________________. "This man from Scotland Yard doesn't look too (4.) ____________, if you ask me." Hudson, feathers ruffled, started to stand up.

Sir Bernard put a hand on his shoulder saying, "I was (5.) __________ by Sir Reginald, director of the C.I.D. at Scotland Yard, that he has given the investigation to his best man. I would like to ask everybody to fully (6.) _____________ with Inspector Hudson."

"Oh! Get on with it, man," spat Penelope Montgomery.
"Yes, where was I? Last week I instructed our financial expert, Mr Charles Greaves, to trace the transactions."
Earl Montgomery interrupted. "So, what did he discover? Who's the guilty person?"
"We still don't know, chairman."
"Why not?"
"Because Charles Greaves has not been seen in the bank since yesterday."
There was an immediate uproar in the meeting room and everybody started talking at once. After a few minutes, Earl Montgomery tapped sharply against his teacup with a teaspoon.
"Order please. I said order!"
His raised voice caused the people to calm down and he said, "Mr Greaves is obviously the guilty party then. If he is such an expert, then he stole the money and is now probably lying on a beach somewhere in South America."

Übung 11: Welche Gegenteile gehören zusammen? Setzen Sie die passende Ziffer ein!

ÜBUNG 11 !

1. raised	☐ innocent
2. calm	☐ first
3. last	☐ nobody

4. guilty — ☐ stormy
5. everybody — ☐ lowered

"With all due respect, sir. I know Greaves very well and he just doesn't seem the type."
"That's humbug, Patterson," the Earl replied. "The mass murderer, Dr. Caine, was also a very nice man, but it didn't stop him killing a lot of people."
Loud conversation broke out again. Hudson had had enough. He stood up and banged with his knuckles on the table. "Ladies and gentlemen. Quiet, please."
The people ignored him, so he grabbed an empty bottle from the table and let it drop with a crash to the floor. There was immediate silence.
"Oops! Sorry about that," said Hudson. "Now, everybody listen to me. This is my investigation and I am in charge. I promise to do my best to apprehend the thief. In order to do this I will need full co-operation from everybody. There is the possibility that Mr Greaves is guilty, but, according to English law, a man is innocent until proven guilty. Sir Bernard, I would now like to have a tour of the bank."
A respectful silence descended on the room and Hudson left followed by Sir Bernard.

ÜBUNG 12 !

Übung 12: Welcher Satz enthält die richtige Zeitform? Kreuzen Sie an!

1. Hudson ist gerade bei seinen Ermittlungen.
   a) ☐ Hudson has investigated.
   b) ☐ Hudson is investigating.

c) ☐ Hudson was investigating.

2. Die Leute haben Hudson ignoriert.
   a) ☐ The people ignored Hudson.
   b) ☐ The people had ignored Hudson.
   c) ☐ The people were ignoring Hudson.

3. Sir Bernard arbeitet seit vielen Jahren bei der Bank.
   a) ☐ Sir Bernard worked at the bank for many years.
   b) ☐ Sir Bernard has worked at the bank for many years.
   c) ☐ Sir Bernard is working at the bank since many years.

4. Gestern um 8 Uhr fuhr Hudson gerade zur Arbeit.
   a) ☐ Yesterday at 8 am, Hudson drove to work.
   b) ☐ Yesterday at 8 am, Hudson is driving to work.
   c) ☐ Yesterday at 8 am, Hudson was driving to work.

"So, what would you like to see first, Inspector?"
Hudson thought about it for a moment. "First you could give me some general information about your headquarters, Sir Bernard. How many people work here and how many departments do you have?"
"We have 69 employees working here. They are divided up into the customer relations department, the loans department and the financial advisory department. However, we don't have to worry about those, because their computers are not capable of making transactions above one thousand pounds. The only departments capable of this are IT, accounts, investments and of course, department heads."
"I see. Let's visit the departments in that order then, shall we?"
They arrived at the IT department where Sir Bernard introduced

Hudson to the department head, Frank Burrows.
"Mr Burrows. Please tell me what the responsibilities of your department are," requested Inspector Hudson.
"Well, sir. We are responsible for anything to do with the computers and their systems. We install all the software and keep it updated. We also install all the hardware and maintain and repair it."
"Have you any idea who has been carrying out the illegal transactions, Mr Burrows?"

ÜBUNG 13 !

Übung 13: Beantworten Sie die Fragen zum Text!

1. How many employees does the bank have?

____

2. Which department do Hudson and Sir Bernard visit first?

____

3. What is the name of Inspector Hudson's boss?

____

4. Who is chairing the emergency meeting?

____

"Not really. It could have been any one of about twenty-five computers. I was rather hoping that Charlie Greaves could have pointed out exactly which computer it was, but I hear he's disappeared."
"That's right. Do you think it was him who stole the money?"
"I don't think he's the type, but I guess it could have been him. On the other hand, it could have been any one of about twenty-five people, myself included."

"Yes, I've thought of that, Mr Burrows. I'll have to ask you to remain available for the next few days. How many people work for you?"
"Three, but we're working day and night trying to trace the computer the transactions were made from."
"Here's my card. If you trace the computer, contact me immediately. I also might have to interview your people within the next few days. Please make sure they know."
Hudson and Sir Bernard left the IT department and made their way to the accounts department.

Übung 14: Lesen Sie weiter und ordnen Sie die Buchstaben in der Klammer zu einem sinnvollen Wort!

"Here we are, Inspector. May I introduce Miss Pelham, head of (1. tacngoucni) ____________________."

"It's a pleasure to meet you Miss Pelham," Hudson said, smiling at the middle-aged, rather plump lady.

"Oh! The (2. eslpraue) ___pleasure___ is all mine, Inspector...?"

"Hudson, Madam. James Hudson from Scotland Yard. Now, would you mind if I asked you a few questions?"

"Certainly not, Inspector Hudson. Fire away."

"How many people work in this (3. tpeamndetr) ___department___?"

"Four, including myself."

"Fine, and what sort of things do you do?"

"Oh! Quite boring stuff really. We're still called bookkeepers, but we should (4. leyrla) __________ be called computer file keepers. We record all purchases and sales, calculate the profits and losses, pay and send (5. oncsieiv) invoices and then prepare everything for the external auditors who come once a year."

"That sounds (6. cliptmeacdo) __________. I don't think I would enjoy being an accountant."

Miss Pelham laughed. "A bookkeeper is not an accountant, (7. tepsrinco) __________. Accountants record cash flows, and the value of liabilities and assets, and they also calculate losses and (8. tforsip) __________ etc. However, their main task is to supply people with information."

"Miss Pelham. Have you any idea who could be stealing money from the bank?"

"I haven't, Inspector. All transactions made by this department must be authorised by me. I can assure you that I'm innocent. As a matter of fact, I was the one who informed Sir Bernard that money was going missing."

"That's right, Inspector," mumbled Sir Bernard.

"Well, Miss Pelham. Could you and your staff please remain available for the next few days? I might have some more questions."

"No problem, Inspector. I've cancelled all holidays until this matter is cleared up."

"Thank you, Miss Pelham."

Übung 15: Lesen Sie weiter und setzen Sie die Infinitive in den Klammern in die korrekte Zeit und Person!

With that, Hudson and Sir Bernard (1. make) made their way to Charlie Greaves' office in the investments department.

"Ah! Hugh, Jeremy, this is Inspector Hudson from Scotland Yard. He's (2. come) come to help us with our current problems. Inspector, may I introduce Hugh Montgomery and Jeremy Paxton, two of our three investment officers."

"Montgomery?" Hudson said. "Are you (3. relate) related to the three Montgomerys I just (4. meet) met in the meeting room?"

"Yes. They are my parents and Penelope is my sister," Hugh Montgomery (5. reply) replied quite pleasantly.

"Why weren't you at the meeting?"

"Well, as you will know by now, we're rather short-staffed at the moment."

"Of course. Charlie Greaves."

Jeremy Paxton (6. stop) stopped tapping his fingers on his desk and said irritably, "is this going to take long? We have lots of work to do, you know."

vermute ich

"Ah! Mr Jeremy Paxton, I presume? What exactly do you do, Mr Paxton?"

"We're investment officers. We analyse and observe the financial markets and stock exchanges world-wide. We look at the track records and then decide whether to buy or sell," explained Paxton in brief.

"That sounds easy enough," stated Hudson.

"It's actually very complicated and requires intense research, making snap decisions and also acting on gut feeling."

"Yes. I am familiar with gut feeling, Mr Paxton. It's also very important for a policeman."

Slipping Montgomery a sly glance, Paxton said. "Well, some of us have it and some of us don't."

"I see," said Hudson, registering the look. "How about Charlie Greaves?"

"Charlie's brilliant. He may look and sound like a nerd, but he's the sharpest investment officer I've ever known. I've really learned a lot from him. I just hope you find him soon. Then he can start doing his own share of the work again."

ÜBUNG 16 !

Übung 16: Unterstreichen Sie den „falschen Freund" und setzen Sie ein alternatives Wort ein!

1. Montgomery and Paxton get 10% provision. ____________
2. Hudson is working on his actual case. ____________
3. Miss Pelham proves all the transactions. ____________
4. Hudson would like to become some water. ____________
5. Jeremy Paxton is a very sensible person. ____________
6. Hudson didn't visit the personal department. ____________

7. The bank spends money for charity. ____________

8. Hudson went to school at the gymnasium. ____________

"Have you any idea why Charlie has disappeared, Mr Paxton?"
"I haven't the foggiest idea. He loves his work, sometimes too much, and he's nuts about his wife. If it wasn't for her, he'd probably be a workaholic."
"And you didn't notice him behaving strangely the last few weeks?"
"Charlie always behaves strangely. He's everyone's idea of a mad professor. If he didn't behave strangely, that would make me worry."
"How about you, Mr Montgomery? Do you have any idea why Charlie went missing?" Montgomery shrugged his shoulders before answering.
"Not really, Inspector. All I know is that he was a little worried about his wife, Janet."
"Why's that?"
"Apparently she's desperate to have children. They have been trying for years, but without success. Of course, she sits at home all day, while Charlie is working, so she must be pretty bored. I suggested getting her a part-time job."
"Right. That's all for now. Thank you gentlemen. Please stay accessible in case I need to talk to you again."

Inspector Hudson and Sir Bernard made their way to the reception area. Hudson was deep in thought and nearly bumped into the tea-lady's tea trolley. Sir Bernard obviously knew the elderly tea-lady very well and asked after her health. As he turned back to Hudson, the expression on the inspector's face said, "I thought tea-ladies became extinct around the same time as the dinosaurs."

Übung 17: Setzen Sie den Dialog fort, indem Sie die folgenden Abschnitte in die richtige Reihenfolge bringen!

1. “Quite a few actually, Sir Bernard. Would it be possible to be given a small office for the next few days? I need to interview more people and I would like to check all the transactions made recently.”
2. “Thank you very much, Sir Bernard. I’ll see you tomorrow then.”
3. “Miss Evans has been with the bank for 45 years now, Inspector. We’ve never had the heart to fire her. When she retires next year, the job will retire with her. Anyway, Inspector, what do you think? Do you have any suspects yet?”
4. “Okay Inspector. Goodbye!”
5. “Absolutely no problem, Inspector.” He glanced at his wrist-watch. “It’s a bit late now, but I can have an office available for you from tomorrow morning. Just ask my secretary.”

Reihenfolge: 3 1 5 2 4

Chapter 3: With a Little Help from My Friends

Hudson drove home to his flat in his old Bentley and was greeted warmly by his housekeeper, Miss Paddington. “Good evening, James. I’ve prepared one of your favourite meals. Shepherds pie! We can eat in twenty minutes.”
Hudson smelled the mouthwatering aroma of his favourite pie, topped with his beloved cheddar cheese. “Wonderful, Miss Paddington. I’ll just have a look at the newspaper while I’m waiting.”

"Take your time, James. Our guest won't arrive for another fifteen minutes."

"*Our* guest, Miss Paddington? Now who might that be?"

Miss Paddington had the decency to blush and stuttered. "Erm! That lovely lady, Ms Elliot rang an hour ago and wanted to speak to you. Anyway, the pie is rather big, so I thought I would kill two birds with one stone and invited her."

"You're not matchmaking again, are you, Miss Paddington?"

"Heaven forbid! She wanted to talk to you, and I had prepared too much pie. It was just a coincidence, James."

"Hmm! You do know how many guilty suspects I have interrogated, Miss Paddington?"

Becoming noticeably flustered, Miss Paddington exclaimed. "Look at the time! I'd better get changed before Ms Elliot arrives."

She dashed out of the kitchen and Inspector Hudson grinned, settling himself into his comfortable old armchair with his paper.

Hudson's grin faded quickly when he read the headlines.

"Heist of the Century at Warminster Bank!"

Hudson immediately tried to call his boss, Sir Reginald, but he wasn't in the office. He then tried calling Sir Bernard's mobile phone, but only heard: "The number you are calling is temporarily unavailable."

"So much for us being contactable twenty-four hours a day," thought Hudson, rather angrily. Someone in the bank must have tipped off the press.

Übung 18: Übersetzen Sie!

1. Miss Paddington steht in der Küche und kocht.

Miss P. is standing in the kitchen cooking

2. Hudson liebt seinen alten Bentley.

____

3. Hudson und Miss Paddington erwarten Besuch.

____

4. Irgendjemand hat der Zeitung einen Tipp gegeben.

____

5. Miss Paddington ist niemals im Ausland gewesen.

____

6. Elvira Elliot will mit Inspector Hudson reden.

____

Hudson decided to send Sir Bernard a text message. He searched through his briefcase, found the instruction booklet for his mobile, and started to follow the instructions, biting his tongue in concentration. He pressed the menu button and selected 'Text Message'. Then he started to enter his message with great difficulty. At that moment, the doorbell rang shrilly and Hudson gave a grunt of frustration. He heard voices and the next moment the door to the living room flew open and Elvira Elliot entered in a cloud of expensive perfume.

"James, hello. What an earth are you doing?"

"Hello Elvira. I'm trying to text Sir Reginald, but this blasted new mobile won't do what I want it to."

"Ah! They must have given you a female one, James. Only joking. Here, give it to me. Now, what would you like to say?"

"Erm! You see, the message is rather confidential, Elvira."

"Oh! Don't be ridiculous. By the time you've figured it out, our pie will be cold. Fire away."

"Okay then. Ask him if he knows, how the press got hold of the Warminster Bank information. We planned to keep it secret and now it's plastered all over the newspapers. No doubt it will also be on the seven o'clock news."

Elvira did some quick shuffling with her right hand for a few seconds, then proudly announced. "Done!"

"How the devil did you do that, Elvira? That was quicker than the eye can see."

"Practice makes perfect, James. Shall we eat?"

Hudson, shaking his head, rose and followed Elvira into the dining room.

! ÜBUNG 19

Übung 19: Lesen Sie weiter und setzen Sie gleichbedeutende Ausdrücke für die Wörter in Klammern ein!

They ate in (1. peace) ________________, concentrating on the delicious taste of the pie. Elvira crossed her knife and fork on the plate, leaned back and (2. said) ________________. "Well, I must say, Miss Paddington, that was the best shepherd's pie that I've eaten in years. You must (3. let me have) ________________ the recipe."

"I'll do that, Ms Elliot. Would you like some apple pie and custard for (4. afters) ________________?"

"Not for me thanks. If I eat that, I'll have to run an (5. extra) ________________ five miles tomorrow to stay in shape."

"I'd love some apple pie and custard, Miss Paddington," said Hudson, feeling rather embarrassed.

"I'll just pop into the kitchen and (6. get it) ________________,"
replied Miss Paddington.

When she had gone, Elvira turned to Hudson. "Now then James. What's all this about the Warminster Bank?"

Hudson (7. rapidly) ________________ explained the case to Elvira. Elvira thought for a while about what James had just told her.

"Well I must say, James, it all sounds very interesting. When do you (8. start) ________________ your investigation?"

"To be honest, I've already started. I just came home from the bank. They've promised me my own office from tomorrow morning onwards."

"So, it all begins in earnest tomorrow morning?"

"Actually, I have an appointment with Charlie's wife, Janet Greaves, at 8 pm. After that I should know more."

"May I come along too James? I promise I won't be a burden. You can introduce me as your assistant."

"Actually, that might not be a bad idea. She must be worried about her husband. It would be good to have you along in case she gets emotional."

"Oh! James!"

They took Hudson's car and drove along Cromwell Road towards Chelsea. Never really comfortable with silences, Hudson said to Elvira, "so, what case are you working on at the moment?"

Übung 20: Welche Wörter gehören zusammen? Tragen Sie die entsprechende Ziffer in die Kästchen ein!

1. insurance	☐ officer
2. bank	☐ agent
3. foreign	☐ confirmation
4. police	☐ clerk
5. sales	☐ currency
6. exchange	☐ representative
7. order	☐ rate

"Actually, I've just wrapped a case up. A gang of thieves were breaking into art galleries all over London. Then they took the paintings to mainland Europe and sold them there on the black market. It took me weeks, going through mountains of paperwork, but then I discovered that one of the mobile security guards was an ex-convict. I had him followed and sure enough, he was caught red-handed, using his pass-key to let the gang into an art gallery in Soho. They were all arrested and now I have a few well-earned days off."

"Good for you, Elvira. With your instincts, you should have joined the police force."

"Is that a job offer, James? Thanks, but no thanks. The police pay peanuts. Besides, when I'm on a case I'm literally my own boss. I couldn't work with an inspector breathing down my neck."

"I hope you don't mean me, Elvira. Oh dear! We appear to be lost!"

"We? James? Surely you mean YOU are lost?"

"Yes, you're right. Can you read a map?"

"Of course I can. I used to be a girl guide, you know."

"It's in the glove compartment. The map light is above it on the dash-board. We're looking... Sorry! I'M looking for Marshall Avenue."

"Got it! Go straight for about 500 yards. At the roundabout, turn right into Harpers Lane, then turn left at the traffic lights."
Hudson obeyed the instructions and within a few minutes they had arrived at the house in Marshall Avenue.

ÜBUNG 21 !

Übung 21: Übersetzen Sie!

1. wrap up a case ______________
2. in the glove compartment ______________
3. We appear to be lost. ______________
4. Turn right at the roundabout. ______________
5. The police pay peanuts. ______________
6. a few well-earned days off ______________

Chapter 4: Mrs Greaves is Paid a Visit

When Mrs Greaves answered the door, she was so pretty that Hudson immediately became tongue-tied.
"Good evening," said Mrs Greaves. "You must be Inspector Hudson from Scotland Yard. Is there any news of my husband, Charlie?"
Hudson blushed. "Well. Erm. You see..."
Elvira came to his rescue. "That's right Mrs Greaves. We're investigating your husband's disappearance. I'm afraid there's no news at the moment. May we come in?"
"I'm sorry. I seem to have forgotten my manners. Yes. Please come in."

The house even had a parlour and as they entered, Hudson pursed his lips at the sight of the obviously very expensive Chippendale furniture. He lowered himself very cautiously into an armchair that had probably cost more than his monthly salary, and Mrs Greaves said, "yes, please take a seat. Would you like something to drink? I have tea, coffee or alcohol, but I assume that you're not permitted to drink on duty, are you?"

Elvira looked a little disappointed. Hudson said, "I'd love a cup of tea, Mrs Greaves. What kind is it?"

"Teeleys, I think. They're the best tea bags I know."

Groaning inwardly, Hudson accepted bravely.

"And you, Miss. What can I get you?"

"Sorry. I didn't introduce myself. My name's Elliot."

"Well, Constable Elliot. What would you like to drink?"

"I'll have a coffee, if it's not too much trouble."

"I only have instant coffee, I'm afraid."

"That will be fine," said Elvira, trying to hide a smile at being called 'Constable.'

Übung 22: Welche Wörter haben eine ähnliche Bedeutung? Tragen Sie die entsprechende Ziffer in die Kästchen ein!

ÜBUNG 22 !

1. instant	☐ dear
2. rescue	☐ save
3. pretty	☐ allowed
4. expensive	☐ immediate
5. salary	☐ carefully
6. cautiously	☐ beautiful
7. permitted	☐ wages

When Mrs Greaves returned with the beverages, they sipped at them politely, doing their best not to grimace.
Placing his mug gently on the unstable-looking coffee table, Hudson started his questioning.
"Mrs Greaves. Have you any idea where your husband could have gone?"
"Certainly not, Inspector. Charlie always comes home. If he's going to be late, he calls me."
"I see. Erm! I must warn you that I will have to ask some very personal questions. Does that bother you?"
"No it doesn't. Ask me anything you like."
"Are you happily married, Mrs Greaves?"
"Yes, I am. Charlie and I love each other very much."
"So you don't have any marital problems?"
"Of course we have arguments, like everybody else. We desperately want to have children. We've been trying for years. The doctor said that there's nothing wrong with me, but Charlie refuses to go to a doctor and get checked out."
"Anything else?"
"Only that Charlie works such long hours and I'm stuck at home. I asked him not to work so hard, but he wouldn't listen. Sometimes I think he loves his job more than me."

ÜBUNG 23 !

Übung 23: Formulieren Sie die Sätze im Passiv!

1. Hudson will question Mrs Greaves later.

....

2. Someone visits Mrs Greaves regularly.

....

3. Someone has kidnapped Charlie Greaves.

---

4. Hudson is speaking to Elvira at the moment.

---

5. She gave Hudson the information.

---

6. Paxton doesn't like other people telling him what to do.

"Mrs Greaves. This is a big house in a very expensive yuppie area. Can you afford the mortgage?"
"Oh yes! Charlie is brilliant with investments. We don't have any financial problems."
"Does your husband have any enemies?"
"You must be joking, inspector. Charlie is the sweetest and most harmless person in the world."
"Right. Well, that's about it, Mrs Greaves. Do you have any questions, Elv... Constable Elliot?"
Covering her mouth with her hand to hide her smile, Elvira said, "Mrs Greaves. Don't you get bored sitting at home all day?"
"I most certainly do. I told Charlie that if I don't get pregnant soon, I would have to get a part-time job, so that I don't die of boredom."
Hudson rose from the armchair saying, "I would like to thank you for being so honest and open, Mrs Greaves. As soon as we hear anything about your husband, we will let you know straight away."
"Thank you Inspector, and you too Constable Elliot. Let me walk you to the front door."
After saying goodbye, Hudson and Elliot dashed through the rain

and hastily got into the car. Hudson tapped the steering wheel a few times.

Übung 24: Lesen Sie weiter und setzen Sie die richtige Präposition in die Lücken ein!
(in 3x, on 2x, out)

"What do you think, Elvira? Was she telling the truth?"

"Mainly, yes. Although I do think that she is hiding something."

"I agree with you (1.) ______ that. What the...?"

They both jumped (2.) ______ shock when there was a loud knock (3.) ______ Hudson's side window. A man was standing there with a coin (4.) ______ his hand, gesturing for Hudson to open his window. Hudson turned the ignition key and lowered the window a few inches.

"You nearly gave me a heart attack. What's the problem?"

"Sorry about that, mister. Are you the police?"

"Yes."

"I thought so. I saw you come (5.) ______ of the Greave's house. I'm their next door neighbour."

"Congratulations."

"No. You don't understand. I read (6.) ______ the newspaper that Charlie has gone missing. I have some valuable information."

On closer inspection, Hudson saw that the man was very lightly dressed and wearing tartan slippers.

"Look. You'd better get in the back seat, before you catch pneumonia."

"I'd rather not. I don't want any of my neighbours to see me, or there will be gossip."

"See here. Get into the back before I lose my temper."

The man climbed reluctantly into the back seat.

"This seat's cold, governor."

"That's because it's leather. Mr...?"

"Harris is the name. Right, how much is this information worth then?"

"I beg your pardon," said Hudson.

"How much will you pay me for the information?"

Übung 25: Lesen Sie weiter und setzen Sie die passenden Wörter in die Lücken ein!

(notebook, arrest, questioning, tough, information, evidence, jiffy, withholding)

ÜBUNG 25 !

Elvira gave the man a hard stare and said: "We don't pay for information. It's your duty as a citizen to help the police with their enquiries. However, if you don't give us the (1.) ______________, I'm afraid we will have to (2.) ______arrest______ you for (3.) ______________ vital (4.) ______________."

"Okay. People on the television always get paid for giving information."

Elvira started tapping some handcuffs into the palm of her hand, trying her best to look (5.) ________________. Hudson realised that she was playing the bad guy, so it was up to him to play the good guy.

"Inspector," he said to Elvira, giving her a wink. "I think you left your (6.) ____________ in the Greaves' house."

"Right, Hudson. I'll be back in a (7.) __________. Mr Harris, stay there. I might want to take you to the Yard for (8.) ____________."

Elvira raced back to the house.
Harris, by now looking worried, said with bravado, "Inspector eh? Well, she doesn't scare me."
"Well, she should. She had a man jailed for 5 years last month. All because he withheld information."
Harris started to fidget, his watery eyes betraying his panic.
"I'll tell you everything, mister. Just keep her away from me."
"I'll try. You had better give me the information. Before she gets back."
"Mrs Greaves has a lover."
"What?"
"It's true, mister. There's a bloke comes twice a week and sneaks in the back door. Anyway, he stays an hour or two and then leaves again."
"Can you give me a description?"
"Not really. He's young, but he always wears a raincoat, hat and sunglasses. I reckon he's murdered Charlie so that he can have his wife."
"What kind of car does he drive?"

"I haven't seen a car. He's normally on foot. Maybe he parks his car on another street."

"Ah! Here comes the inspector. Thanks Mr Harris, you've been a big help."

Elvira got into the car waving her notebook and said, "Mr Harris. Are you ready to go to the station now?"

Harris started to stutter.

"I told this nice man everything, Inspector, honest. Please don't lock me up."

"Right. Off you go then. But remember. I'll be watching you!"

Harris dived out of the car and scurried along the footpath to his house.

Elvira looked at James with a raised eyebrow and they both burst out laughing.

"That was the most fun I've had in a long time, Elvira. Are you sure you don't want to join the police?"

"Well, James," said Elvira with a smile, "I just might. I've only been working for the police for one hour, and I've gone from Constable to Inspector. I must be what people call a 'high flyer'. It's getting late. Drive me home, CONSTABLE Hudson."

"Okay Boss."

Übung 26: Was ist richtig: ***much*** *oder* ***many****? Unterstreichen Sie!*

ÜBUNG 26 !

1. How many/much money was stolen?
2. How many/much people live in Hudson's flat?
3. Hudson doesn't have many/much time to solve the case.
4. How many/much hours has Elvira worked for the police?
5. Does Hudson get many/much information from Mr Harris?
6. How many/much times did Hudson ring the doorbell?

The next morning Hudson went to Scotland Yard very early and ran a computer check on all the people under suspicion. Sir Bernard, Jeremy Paxton and the Montgomerys all appeared to have financial problems. It was also possible that Charlie Greaves arranged his own disappearance, after finding out that his wife had a lover. After careful consideration, Hudson became convinced that the solution to the case could probably be found somewhere within the bank's documents. He called Sir Reginald's extension and was quite surprised when his boss answered the phone at such an early hour.

"Good morning, Sir Reginald. You're in the office bright and early."

"Morning old boy. Yes. I've been here all night trying to find out how the case could have been leaked to the press."

"Have you had any luck?"

"The only thing I can say for sure is that it wasn't leaked from the Yard. I assume it was someone in the bank."

"I think you're right, Sir. I'd like to come up and see you, if you have five minutes?"

"Of course, Inspector. My secretary isn't in yet, I'm afraid. All I can offer you is instant coffee."

"That's fine, sir. I'll be up in a jiffy."

ÜBUNG 27 !

Übung 27: Lesen Sie weiter und setzen Sie die richtige Präposition in die Lücken ein!

Remembering his keep fit campaign, Hudson took the stairs instead (1.) ______ the lift to Sir Reginald's floor.

"Ah! There you are, Hudson. White (2.) ______ two sugars, wasn't it?"

"That's right. Thank you very much, sir."

"Now then. How's your investigation proceeding?"

Hudson brought Sir Reginald up (3.) ___to___ date and concluded by saying that he thought the answer would be found (4.) ___in___ the bank's documentation.

"The problem is, Sir Reginald, the bank has a great amount (5.) ___on___ documentation. I'm a police inspector, not an auditor, so I will need some help."

"Right, Inspector. Well, I suppose I could lend you Constable Richards for a few days."

"Forgive me for saying this sir, but Constable Richards isn't the right type for this detail. I need an expert."

"Inspector. Do you expect me to produce an economic expert from (6.) ______ my sleeve?"

"Of course not sir. I know of such an expert, who would be available (7.) ______ a few days."

"You do? Now who would that be?"

"Elvira Elliot, sir."

"Elvira Elliot? She's an insurance agent."

"She is, sir. She's also the best document investigator that I know."

"Hmm! That sounds like a good idea. We could offer her a short, freelance, consultancy contract. Has she agreed to do this?"

"She doesn't even know about it, sir. However, I'm pretty sure that she will say yes."

"Fine, Hudson. Just clear it with personnel, before she starts working for us."
"Thanks sir. You won't regret it."
"I hope not, Hudson. I hope not."
Hudson returned to his office and placed a call to Elvira Elliot.
"549 7122. Whoever you are, I hope you have a very good reason for calling me at 7 am."
"Good morning Elvira. It's James."
"James? James Hudson?"

! ÜBUNG 28

Übung 28: Formulieren Sie die Sätze in indirekter Rede!

1. "Elvira's an insurance agent." (he)

He said Elvira was an insurance agent.

2. "She's the best document investigator I know." (he)

____

3. "That sounds like a good idea." (she)

____

4. "You won't regret it." (he)

____

5. "I hope not." (she)

____

"Yes. Look, I'm sorry for waking you so early, but I'm in a bit of a dilemma."
"So, what's the problem then?"

Hudson explained about his conversation with Sir Reginald and the authorisation to employ her.

"I'd really love to help you James, but I do need some rest and recuperation."

"I've spoken to personnel. The fee would be three hundred pounds per day, plus expenses."

There was a moment of silence.

"Elvira? Are you still there?"

"When do I start?"

"Let's meet at Warminster Bank at nine. I can fill you in on the details then."

"Right. I'll take the tube. Could you give me a lift to your place afterwards? I need to collect my car."

"No problem. I'll see you at nine then. Oh! Elvira?"

"Yes, James?"

"Thanks. You're a pal." Freund

"Don't mention it, James. Bye."

Übung 29: Stellen Sie Hudson folgende Fragen auf Englisch!

ÜBUNG 29 !

1. Sie fragen ihn, wann Sie anfangen können zu arbeiten.

2. Sie wollen von ihm wissen, wie lang seine Ermittlung andauern wird.

3. Sie fragen Hudson, ob er schon mit Frau Greaves gesprochen hat.

4. Sie fragen ihn, ob er fünf Minuten Zeit für Sie hat.

---

5. Sie fragen den Inspector nach seiner Lieblingsteesorte.

When Inspector Hudson arrived at the bank just before 9 am, Sir Bernard was waiting for him in the reception area.
"Good morning, Inspector."
"Good morning, Sir Bernard."
"I've had an office cleared for you. It's a little small, I'm afraid, but it has all the equipment you will need."
"I'm very grateful, Sir Bernard."
"My pleasure, Inspector. Shall we go and look at it?"
"If we could wait a few minutes, sir. I'm expecting my assistant to arrive any minute. Ah! There she is."
Elvira Elliot entered wearing a very elegant, black business suit.
"Sir Bernard. Allow me to introduce my assistant, Inspector Elliot. Inspector Elliot, Sir Bernard Patterson."
Obviously very impressed, Sir Bernard bowed, took Elvira's right hand in his and pretended to kiss it.
"Welcome to our humble bank, Inspector Elliot."
Sir Bernard escorted them to the small office on the ground floor, gave Hudson the key and rushed off for a 9 am appointment.

Übung 30: Welche Berufsbezeichnung ist gemeint? Setzen Sie ein!

1. a bank employee who advises clients how to increase their money

---

2. a person who welcomes people to a company

---

3. a person who records all financial incomings and outgoings

---

4. a person who drives a car which is for hire

---

5. a person who lives in and looks after people in their own home

---

6. a person who corresponds and communicates on behalf of their boss

---

Elvira raised a questioning eyebrow.
"Inspector Elliot?"
"Well, I couldn't demote you, could I? You're actually earning more than an inspector does. I should really have said Chief Inspector."
"That would mean that I am your superior!"
"Be careful, Elvira. I'm in charge of this case."
"Yes Master!"
"So, let's see what we have here. It is very small, isn't it? I think they must have cleared out a cleaning cupboard."
"Beggars can't be choosers, James."
"Well at least we have a telephone and a computer. I wonder if we are online?"
"I should think so. There's a cable going from the computer to the telephone socket."

"What's this, Elvira?"
"That's a Dictaphone, James. If you press this button here, it records everything you say."

ÜBUNG 31 !

Übung 31: Lesen Sie weiter und unterstreichen Sie alle Begriffe, die mit dem Computer zu tun haben!

"I think we have everything we need, Elvira. The printer has a scanner and a facsimile machine integrated and there's even one of those new, complicated coffee machines in the corner. Can you think of anything else?"
"Look James," said Elvira from the computer terminal, "the bank has its own intranet. I bet we could access all the files through this."
"Super."
"Well, there is one problem. We need a password to gain entry. I'll go and ask the receptionist to get it for me. I'll also ask her to provide another office chair for you."

"Right Elvira. I'll wait for you then."
"Oh no you don't, James. Somebody called me very early today, so I haven't had anything to eat or drink yet."
"Miss Paddington prepared a big lunch box. You know she always makes too much."
"Great. So by the time I get back, you should have coffee ready. Make mine a cappuccino."
"But I'm not sure that I know how to make coffee. Miss Paddington always does that kind of thing for me."
"James. I hope that I'm never stranded on a desert island with you. Just do it. I'm sure you'll manage."
"Right. One cappuccino, coming right up."

Übung 32: Übersetzen Sie!

1. Wir benötigen ein Passwort, um Zugang zu erlangen.

____

2. Hudson macht Kaffee, während Elvira den Stuhl holt.

____

3. Das Büro hat alles, was sie brauchen.

____

4. Elvira möchte gern einen Cappuccino trinken.

____

5. James hat vergessen die Kaffeemaschine anzuschließen.

____

6. Sie werden Zugang zum Intranet bekommen.

____

Elvira returned carrying a chair fifteen minutes later, and found Hudson standing in front of the coffee machine, scratching his head.
"What seems to be the problem, James?"
"I can't get this darned coffee machine to work. I followed all the instructions precisely. I filled up the water, put in the coffee beans, put the plastic pipe into the milk carton and pressed all the right buttons, but nothing is happening."
Elvira looked behind the machine.
"James?"
"Yes Elvira?"

"I think it would be a good idea if we plugged it in!"
"Oh! Bother!"

Übung 33: Lesen Sie weiter und ergänzen Sie den Dialog mit den vorgegebenen Wörtern!
(preparing, electronic, produced, breakfast, paperwork, seems, password, computer)

Within minutes Elvira had the coffee ready and they started their working (1.) ________________.

Between bites, Hudson asked, "did you get the (2.) ____________?"

"I certainly did. I suggest that I work through the (3.) ____________ files, as we only have one (4.) ________________. You could visit the different departments and go through the existing (5.) ______________."

"Good idea. I'll get started as soon as I've finished my coffee."

As Hudson was (6.) ________________ to leave, there was the muffled sound of 'God Save the Queen'.

Hudson said, "What's that?"

"I've no idea, James, but it (7.) ______________ to be coming from your overcoat."

Hudson searched his overcoat pockets and (8.) ______________ his mobile phone.

"James! I don't believe it. You have 'God Save the Queen' as your mobile melody?"
"I didn't programme that in," said Hudson, rather flustered. "It must be Sir Reginald's idea of a joke."

Chapter 5: An Invitation to Dinner

While Elvira giggled, he pressed the green answer button.
"Hallo. Inspector Hudson, Scotland Yard. Who's speaking please?"
"Good morning, Hudson. This is Lady Montgomery. We met in the boardroom yesterday. Do you remember?"
"How could I forget, Lady Montgomery? Good morning to you too. What can I do for you?"
"I wanted to apologise for indicating that you were incompetent yesterday."
"Well that's very noble of you, Lady Montgomery."
"Inspector. I would like to invite you for dinner at Montgomery Castle this evening. I won't take no for an answer."
"Well, I am rather busy, Lady Montgomery."
"Oh, it will be work-related, Inspector. We have information that might help you to solve your case."
"In that case Lady Montgomery, I'll gladly come. I might have to bring my assistant along though."

ÜBUNG 34 !

*Übung 34: Formulieren Sie die Fragen mit **what if**!*

1. Do you think Hudson will catch the guilty party?

What if Hudson caught the guilty part?

2. Would it be a problem for you to make coffee?

____

3. Do the bank employees know Elvira is an insurance agent?

____

4. Can you believe that Charlie Greaves is the thief?

____

5. Can you imagine Hudson not solving a case?

____

6. Do you mind doing all these exercises?

____

"Absolutely not a problem, Inspector. We dine at eight sharp."
"Lady Montgomery, just let me note down the address. Montgomery Castle, you said?"
"That's right, Inspector. Just take Kingsland Road out of the city. When you get to Stoke Newington, turn left at the Red Bull pub onto Lake Road. After two miles, you will see the Castle gates on your right. Have you got that?"
"Yes, I've got that, Lady Montgomery. I will do my best to be punctual."
"Don't do your best to be punctual, Inspector. Be punctual! Goodbye."
"Goodbye, Lady Montgomery."

When Hudson explained, Elvira agreed to accompany him. Agreeing to meet in the canteen at 12 o'clock for lunch, Hudson left the office.

Inspector Hudson made his way to the IT department. "Good morning Inspector. We spoke yesterday. Frank Burrows."
"Good morning, Mr Burrows. Could you show me where you keep your paper files please? I need to do some snooping."
"Certainly, Inspector. Your nice colleague just rang. I gave her some access codes for the database and filing system."
"Good man, Mr Burrows. Lead the way please."
"Right, here we are, Inspector. I don't think that you'll have much fun though. Most of the stuff in the files is IT-related. You know, hardware, software, spare parts for the computers, and so on."
"Thanks, Mr Burrows. I'll just browse through and let you know if I need anything."
"Sure thing. I'll be in my office."

Übung 35: Lesen Sie weiter und unterstreichen Sie die Verben in der Verlaufsform!

After a couple of hours of looking through files that he could hardly understand, Hudson was starting to get a headache. Glancing at his watch, he saw that it was 11:45 and decided to make his way to the canteen to meet Elvira. After thanking Mr Burrows, he made his way to the ground floor, remembering to use the stairs. Elvira was already waiting for him in the canteen and eating a very small salad.

"Can I get you anything from the buffet, Elvira?"
"A still mineral water would be nice, James."
"Coming up," said Hudson. He got himself a "Ploughman's Lunch" and returned to the table. The canteen was almost empty, giving them a chance to talk.

"How did it go this morning, Elvira?"
"I'm just getting the hang of it, James. It's quite a complicated system. My eyes were getting tired, so I stopped five minutes ago."
"Yes, That's understandable, Elvira."
"I have a couple of things that I want to trace this afternoon. I think the clue is in there somewhere."
"The IT department was completely unsuccessful, I'm afraid. I'm going to the accounts department after lunch."
"What time will we have to leave for Montgomery Castle this evening?"
"Well I'm terrified of being late, so let's leave about seven."
"Could you run me home first? I'd like to get changed."
"Whatever for? You look smashing."
"You wouldn't understand, James. It's a woman thing."
"Oh!"

ÜBUNG 36 !

Übung 36: Welche Wörter gehören in die Lücken? Lesen Sie weiter und setzen Sie die Wörter in der Klammer ein!
(beginning, reward, department, containing, something, relevant, files, schoolgirl)

After lunch, Hudson went to the accounts (1.) ________________.

Miss Pelham greeted him cordially. As a (2.) ________________ he gave her his most charming smile and she blushed like a (3.) ________________.

"Miss Pelham. I'd like to look at your (4.) ________________, if I may?"

"I'll just clear this desk for you, Inspector. Now, which files can I get for you?"

"If it's not too much bother, I'd like the files (5.) ______________ bank transfers for the last three months."

"All the files start on the first of April, Inspector. That's the (6.) ______________ of our fiscal year. Is that all right?"

"That's just fine, Miss Pelham."

Miss Pelham quickly collected the (7.) ______________ files and placed them on the desk, giving Hudson a coy smile.

"Here you are, Inspector. Before you start, would you like (8.) ______________ to drink?"

"No thanks, Miss Pelham. I just had lunch."
"What a pity, I've just made a pot of my favourite Earl Grey."
"One moment, Miss Pelham. Did you just say Earl Grey?"
"Yes I did, Inspector."
"I'd love a cup."
Miss Pelham hurried off blushing, and soon returned with a cup of steaming tea and some chocolate biscuits. Hudson savoured the aroma, took a careful sip and rolled his eyes with pleasure.
"Miss Pelham?"
"Yes, Inspector?"
"Are you by any chance a member of the Red Cross?"
"I'm not quite sure that I understand, Inspector," Miss Pelham answered slightly confused.
"You just saved my life!"

ÜBUNG 37 !

Übung 37: Welches Wort ist das „schwarze Schaf"?

1. policeman, insurance agent, worker, bank manager
2. desk, filing cabinet, desk lamp, bookshelf
3. floppy disk, modem, scanner, printer
4. business card, diary, calendar, Dictaphone
5. owe, credit, loan, overdraft
6. scooter, bicycle, car, motorbike

Hudson perused the files. He soon came across large transactions that had been carried out over the past couple of months. Unfortunately, there wasn't any names on the transfer confirmations, only a code number. He photocopied the relevant pages and placed them in his briefcase. Looking around, he noticed that the office was empty, apart from Miss Pelham.

He approached her desk and said, "Miss Pelham, how come your staff have finished work so early? And why are you wearing your raincoat in the office?"

Smiling shyly, Miss Pelham said, "I've only been waiting for you, Inspector. It's quarter to seven, you know."

"What! Oh my goodness! I'm going to be late for dinner. See you tomorrow, Miss Pelham."

ÜBUNG 38 !

Übung 38: Sind die folgenden Sätze grammatikalisch korrekt? Markieren Sie mit richtig ✔ oder falsch – !

1. They were speaking over the transactions. ☐
2. Miss Pelham was wearing her raincoat. ☐
3. The staff have just finished work. ☐
4. Hudson has visited Mrs Greaves yesterday. ☐

5. Elvira works on the database now. ☐
6. Hudson can't be late for dinner. ☐

With that, he ran down to the reception area. Elvira was flipping through a glossy magazine, a shopping bag next to her chair.
"Elvira! I'm so sorry. I completely lost track of the time."
"I guessed as much, James. I decided to play it safe and went shopping an hour ago. Mind you, I'm going to have to change in the back of your car, en route to the castle."
"Right. Let's go. I hate to think what would happen if we showed up late for dinner."
"Maybe the castle has a torture chamber, James."
"Don't say that, Elvira. It probably has and if it does, she probably uses it."
They took the stairs to the underground garage, where a parking spot had been generously provided by Sir Bernard.

Übung 39: Bringen Sie die Wörter in die richtige Reihenfolge!

ÜBUNG 39 !

1. invited are dinner to they

____

2. overcoat grabbed he briefcase and his

____

3. for mustn't dinner late be we

____

4. was the chairing Montgomery meeting Lord

____

5. the decided take Hudson to stairs

____

6. an went ago Elvira hour shopping

____

Driving along Kingsland Road, Hudson was intrigued by the soft rustling coming from the back of the car. He fought his instinct to adjust the rear view mirror and concentrated on his driving.
“Oh, blast! I forgot the note with the directions.”
There was the sound of a zip being pulled up.
“Where are we, James?”
“We’re in Stoke Newington. I need to fill up anyway. I can ask directions at the next petrol station.”
“Good idea, James. Then I can sit up front with you. It’s bad enough that I’m on a Chief Inspector’s salary. I wouldn’t want people to think that you are my chauffeur.”
“Very funny, Elvira. Ah! There’s a petrol station.”
Hudson pulled up to the petrol pump and was greeted by a skinny old man in blue overalls.
“Evening your Lordship.”
“Just fill her up please.”

ÜBUNG 40 !

Übung 40: Bringen Sie Inspector Hudsons Vorgehensweise in der Bank in eine logische Reihenfolge!

1. visit the IT department
2. meet Sir Bernard
3. visit the investment department

4. go to reception
5. visit the accounts department
6. attend the meeting

Reihenfolge: _ _ _ _ _ _

The petrol pump attendant nodded and commenced filling the car. Suddenly his mouth dropped open and he muttered, "Cor Blimey!" Hudson followed the line of his eyes and saw a very beautiful woman walking across the forecourt and entering the shop.
The old man replaced the petrol cap and said, "That will be fifty pounds, sir."
Hudson sighed at the expense, removed his wallet and paid.
"I wonder if you could help us? We're looking for Montgomery Castle."
"That's easy, sir. See that pub two hundred yards down the road?"
"Yes."
"Well, turn left there onto Lake Road. The entrance to the castle is about two miles down, on the right."
"Lovely. Thanks very much."
"Could I ask you something, sir?"
"Sure."
"Well just now you said us and we?"
"That's right. My passenger is in the back."
"The back's empty, sir."
"Impossible!"
Just then they both heard a wolf-whistle and turned their heads to see that the woman had come out of the shop and was walking towards them. Hudson couldn't believe his eyes. It was Elvira Elliot wearing a very sleek evening gown and patent leather high heels. The petrol pump attendant scurried around the car and held

the passenger door open for her. Elvira rewarded him with a smile, got in the car and said, “Flies, James.”
“Uh!”
“If you don’t close your mouth, flies will get in it.”
“Uh!”
“James. It’s twenty to eight. Let’s go!”
Hudson drove the rest of the way in a trance.

Chapter 6: Arrival at Montgomery Castle

! ÜBUNG 41

Übung 41: Lesen Sie weiter und setzen Sie die passenden Wörter in die Lücken ein!
(fortune, illuminated, told, going to, look at, noticed)

Ten minutes later they arrived at Montgomery Castle. The driveway (1.) ________________ the castle was about a mile long, but the gardens appeared to be neglected. As they drove through an avenue of trees, the (2.) ________________ castle appeared. Hudson’s trained eyes (3.) ________________ the neglect here too. Only one wing of the castle was lit.
“It must cost a (4.) ________________ in upkeep,” thought Hudson.
A butler, who appeared to be as old as the castle itself, was waiting for them at the entrance.
“Good evening, madam, sir. Could I (5.) ________________ your invitation please?”

"I'm afraid we don't have one," Hudson replied. "Inspectors Elliot and Hudson of Scotland Yard. We were invited by Lady Montgomery by telephone."

"Of course. Lady Montgomery (6.) ____________ me of your imminent arrival."

"Can we come in then?" enquired Elvira. "It's a little chilly out here without a jacket."
"Most certainly, madam. The family are having an aperitif in the library. Please walk this way."
They followed the butler from the reception hall, down a long corridor, the walls lined with ancestral portraits. The butler was walking extremely slowly and Hudson hoped that they weren't going to be late. At precisely one minute to eight, they entered the library.

The butler tried his best to stand to attention, and announced, "My Lords, Ladies and Gentlemen."
Hudson glanced around, but there were only two people in the room.
"Announcing Inspectors Elliot and Hudson of Scotland Yard, London."
Lady Montgomery rose from her chair, motioning to the butler to leave.
"All right Nigel. You've done your duty. You can go and help cook now."
"Yes, Lady Montgomery."
"Now then, Inspector. Hudson, wasn't it?"
"Yes madam."
"And who is this lovely creature that you have brought with you?

Not your colleague, surely?"
Lady Montgomery's eyes made a quick, hard assessment of Elvira Elliot.
"Yes it is. May I introduce Inspector Elliot. We are working together on this case."
"Pleased to meet you, Inspector Elliot. Personally, I believe that women belong at home, looking after the family and household."
Elvira bristled. "I've never been married, Lady Montgomery."
"Oh, you poor girl. Oh, well. You still might get lucky."
Hudson saw that Elvira was starting to shake with anger. When she started to open her mouth to give Lady Montgomery a piece of her mind, he nudged her quickly in the ribs.

! ÜBUNG 42

Übung 42: In die folgenden Sätze hat sich ein Fehler eingeschlichen. Schreiben Sie die Sätze richtig auf!

1. Hudson brought Elvira to Montgomery Castle.

____

2. The butler has made his duty.

____

3. On the way to the castle, they were stopping for petrol.

____

4. Elvira has been looking very elegant tonight.

____

5. It costed Hudson a lot of money to fill up his car.

____

6. Elvira had been getting very angry.

____

"Richard, I think you know Inspector Hudson already. This other police officer is Inspector...?"
"Elliot," growled Elvira.
"Hudson, welcome. And a very special welcome to you, my dear."
The sound of a gong interrupted the greetings and Hudson and Elliot were escorted into the dining room.
Lord Montgomery insisted on escorting Elvira. Hudson was not a happy man. He also noticed that Lady Montgomery didn't seem too pleased either.
The dining room was huge. The dining table could seat forty people. Elvira looked gratefully at the roaring fire blazing in the hearth and thought, this room is bigger than my flat!
The meal was a little rich for Hudson's taste, but he bravely ate a polite amount.

Übung 43: Setzen Sie die Wörter in Klammern in die Lücken ein!
(rumours, convinced, surprised, politely, conclusive, concerning, conclusion, handle)

Afterwards, they retired to the parlour for brandy and cigars. Hudson (1.) ____________________ refused both.

"Lady Montgomery," he said, "you indicated on the telephone that you have some information (2.) ____________________ the case?"

"That's right, Inspector."

Lord Montgomery looked (3.) ________________.

"Do we, Margaret?"

"Oh, shut up Richard. Let me (4.) ________________ this."

"Yes, dear."

"Now, were was I? Charlie Greaves is your man, Inspector."

"What brings you to that (5.) ____________, Lady Montgomery?"

"Well, it's obvious, isn't it? My son Hugh told me of (6.) ________________ that his wife is having an affair."

"That isn't really (7.) ________________ evidence, Lady Montgomery."

"That's true, Inspector. But an hour ago, Burrows from the IT department rang and told my husband that the money transfers were made from Greaves' computer."

"That's true," said Lord Montgomery.

Hudson wasn't (8.) ________________.

"Yes, but. Anyone with access to the computer could have made those transfers."
"Not without Greaves' personal password," said Elvira.
During the drive home, Hudson asked Elvira what she thought.
"It all sounds too simple, James. I've heard the employees at the bank talking about Charlie Greaves and it's all good. On the other hand, it does look as though his wife is seeing someone. That could turn a nice person nasty."
"Yes, I've seen that happen a few times."

Elvira continued. "The Montgomery family seems too good to be true. Despite appearances, I think they're pretty broke. They have a good reason for stealing 25 million."

Übung 44: Übersetzen Sie!

ÜBUNG 44 !

1. Lady Montgomery ist nicht sehr nett.

2. Hudson fühlt sich im Schloss nicht sehr wohl.

3. Elvira wird langsam wütend.

4. Das Esszimmer ist größer als Elviras Wohnung.

5. Lady Montgomery versucht Hudson zu beeinflussen.

"Elvira, I don't have a good feeling about Jeremy Paxton either. He's too shifty."
"Yes, you're right, James. I observed him in the canteen today. He certainly acts as though he's hiding something."
"The only other person I can think of is Sir Bernard."
"Oh no, James. Not that sweet old gentleman. Mind you, I bet it turns out to be the butler or the cleaning lady."
"I don't think so, Elvira. Look, before you go to the bank tomor-

row, could you use your connections from your insurance agent's job and do a financial check on all our suspects?"
"Will do, James. They don't usually start work until nine though, so I'll probably be late getting to the bank."
"That's okay, Elvira. I'll have a coffee waiting for you."
They pulled up outside Hudson's flat. With a wink and a smile Elvira said, "Don't forget the plug, James."
As he growled, she scurried to her car, got in, gave a toot of her horn and drove off.

ÜBUNG 45 !

Übung 45: Finden Sie die Synonyme zu den untenstehenden Wörtern im folgenden Absatz!

1. gone ______________
2. right ______________
3. extracted ______________
4. reached ______________
5. tell ______________

The next morning Hudson arrived at the bank at nine sharp and immediately went to see Mr Burrows in the IT department.
"Good morning, Mr Burrows."
"Good morning, Inspector. What can I do for you?"
"Is it true that the transfers were made from Greaves' computer?"
"Yes, Inspector. I went to your office to inform you, but you and your colleague had just left."
"Well, you could have phoned me, Mr Burrows."
"I'm afraid not, sir. I don't have your number."

Hudson pulled out his wallet and gave Burrows his business card. "Here, Mr Burrows."

Burrows took out his mobile phone. As quick as a flash, he entered Hudson's telephone numbers into his mobile's address book.
Shaking his head, Hudson gave a big sigh of frustration.
"The next time, please inform me before anybody else. Okay?"
"Yes, Inspector. I promise."
"Right. I'll be in my office for the next hour, then I'll be in the investments department."
"Right you are, Inspector."

Übung 46: Setzen Sie die richtigen Präpositionen ein!

ÜBUNG 46 !

Hudson returned to his office and set (1.) ______ the coffee machine. He spent the half hour before Elvira's arrival (2.) ______ deep contemplation.

"Good Morning, James. That coffee smells good."

"Coming up, madam. Did you manage (3.) ______ do the check?"

"Yes I did. Now, I have some good news and some bad news. Which would you like first?"

"The good news, please."

"All right. The good news is that I found pretty serious financial problems."

"That's great! And the bad news?"

"The bad news is, that apart (4.) ______ Charlie Greaves, they all have financial problems."

"Oh no," Hudson groaned. "Even your sweet old gentleman, Sir Bernard?"

"Yes, even him. Look, I've brought you the print-outs. Their total debts are (5.) ______ the bottom (6.) ______ the right hand column."

Hudson whistled softly and put the sheets (7.) ______ his briefcase.

"Good job, Elvira. Oh, by the way, Miss Paddington gave me some sandwiches for you. She reckons you don't eat enough."
"Oh, that's very sweet. Thank her for me, will you James?"
"Sure. I'm off to Investments now. Could you continue your research from yesterday? You never know, you just might hit gold."
"Will do, skipper. Lunch in the canteen again?"
"It's a date."
Hudson made his way to the investments department. He didn't really need to go through the files, as he had the confirmation print-outs from the electronic transactions. However, he was very interested in observing Hugh Montgomery and Jeremy Paxton for a few hours.

ÜBUNG 47 !

Übung 47: Beantworten Sie die Fragen zum Text!

1. Who gave Hudson sandwiches?

____

2. Did Elvira have good news or bad news for Hudson?

____

3. Where do Hudson and Elliot have lunch?

---

4. Why couldn't Mr Burrows phone Hudson?

---

5. Who acts as though he is hiding something?

Hugh Montgomery greeted him politely.
"Good morning, Inspector. How may I be of assistance to you?" he asked.
"Morning, Mr Montgomery. I'd like to go through your files, if I may?"
"Most certainly, Inspector. I'll get them for you. You can sit at Charlie's desk, if you like."
"Thanks."

After a few minutes Montgomery returned with the documents.
"Here you are, Inspector. Coffee?"
"No, thanks." But instead of studying the files in detail, Hudson started to interrogate Hugh Montgomery. "Where's Mr Paxton today?"
"Oh, Jeremy quite often shows up late. He has problems getting out of bed in the morning."
"I see."
"I'm sorry I couldn't join you for dinner last night, Inspector. My sister and I were taking care of a pregnant mare, who suddenly went into labour."
"And are mare and foal all right?"
"Just fine, Inspector."

Übung 48: Was wird hier beschrieben? Setzen Sie die Wörter in Klammern ein!
(investment, research, pregnant, invitation, files, investigation)

1. the process of trying to catch a criminal ____________________
2. being asked to dinner ____________________
3. spending money to try and make more ____________________
4. paper records kept in a binder ____________________
5. expecting a baby ____________________
6. discover facts or information ____________________

"Tell me, Mr Montgomery. How is your working relationship with Greaves and Paxton?"
"Well, to be honest, Inspector, Charlie Greaves is a scatter-brain. You know, always losing things. He hardly has any common sense, but he's brilliant at his job. Everybody loves Charlie."
"You don't seem too worried about his disappearance?"
"Oh, I am a little worried. Although I wouldn't be surprised if he showed up soon. He's probably got lost somewhere."
"Interesting, Mr Montgomery. And Paxton?"
"Jeremy is rather the opposite to Charlie, unfortunately. He's your born pessimist. He's always seeing the negative things, which can sometimes get on one's nerves. He's also a bit of a hermit."
"How do you mean?"
"Consider this, Inspector. The three of us have been working together for years now. After all this time, we still don't know a thing about Jeremy's private life."
"That is unusual."

Übung 49: Wie lautet die richtige Antwort? Kreuzen Sie an!

1. How do you do?
   a) ☐ I'm fine thanks.
   b) ☐ How do you do?

2. What do you do?
   a) ☐ I'm a banker.
   b) ☐ I'm learning English.

3. What is Hudson doing?
   a) ☐ He's an inspector.
   b) ☐ He's investigating.

4. The mare has had a foal.
   a) ☐ Where has it gone?
   b) ☐ Congratulations!

Jeremy Paxton burst into the office, shaking raindrops from his umbrella. When he saw Inspector Hudson, he mumbled a barely audible 'good morning'.

"Is it still raining, Mr Paxton?" Hudson asked.

"What do you think, Inspector. This isn't sweat, you know. I hate English weather."

"Sorry. It was a stupid question."

Hudson busied himself with the files, thinking, "This man has got a chip on his shoulder."

Hugh Montgomery looked at Hudson and shrugged his shoulders, as if to say, "I told you so."

"How come you're late to the office again, Jeremy, late night?"

"That's none of your business, Hugh."

Montgomery sighed. “Sir Bernard strongly suggested that we go through Charlie’s diary and portfolios, to ensure that no important customers are neglected. Let’s divide them up. Would you like to work on the diary or the portfolios?”
“Neither.” Jeremy Paxton didn’t even try to be polite and continued, “I’m paid to do one job here, not two. Besides, it’s not in my job description.”
Hudson was starting to enjoy this.

ÜBUNG 50 !

Übung 50: Übersetzen Sie!

1. Abteilungsleiter ____________________
2. Vorstandsvorsitzender ____________________
3. Protokoll ____________________
4. Empfangsperson ____________________
5. Diktiergerät ____________________

“Oh, come on Jeremy. Don’t split hairs. We have to do our best until Charlie’s back. How often has he stood in for you when you’ve been sick or on holiday?”
“Look, Hugh. We all stand in for each other. But I don’t see why I should do Charlie’s work, when he’s run off with 25 million.”
“What! You honestly believe that Charlie ran off with the money?”
“Let’s face it, Hugh. I heard on the grapevine that the money was transferred from Charlie’s computer. If it wasn’t Charlie, it could have been only one of two people, in my book.”
“Me or you?”
“Correct. And I know it wasn’t me!”

"That's ridiculous, Jeremy. Anyone can walk into this office day or night."
"But not anyone could figure out the password. You're Charlie's mate. So I reckon you have more chance than anyone of figuring it out."
Hudson was by now completely ignoring the files. "The plot thickens," he thought.

Übung 51: Bringen Sie die Wörter in die richtige Reihenfolge und bilden Sie sinnvolle Fragen!

! ÜBUNG 51

1. work officers as many investment people how?

____

2. and Hudson up have Elliot teamed?

____

3. ever London it in does rain?

____

4. favourite what tea is Hudson's?

____

5. accounts the head who of is department?

____

"Oh, yeah," Montgomery said, getting noticeably angry. "And what about all these rumours about you I hear, that you're heavily in debt and hanging out in some pretty shady places?"
Now Paxton was getting loud.

"How about you and your precious family, Hugh, old boy? I hear that you are in danger of losing your little castle. Surely what you and your father earn here at the bank doesn't even cover the heating bills? Not to mention the cost of your sister's horses and your mother's servants."

Hudson had heard enough.

"Mr Paxton, Mr Montgomery. Please sit and calm down. Throwing insults at each other will not solve anything. I'll take Charlie's diary and let you know as soon as I have found anything of interest."

ÜBUNG 52 !

Übung 52: Setzen Sie die Verben in Klammern in die richtige Zeitform!

Hudson (1. go) ___________ back to the office he (2. share) ___________ with Elvira.

"How's it going, Elvira?"

"I'm nearly through the whole database, James. No clues yet, I'm afraid."

Hudson (3. tell) ___________ her about the argument he (4. have) ___________ just listened to.

"It sounds as though they don't (5. like) ___________ each other," commented Elvira.

"I don't think Paxton (6. like) ___________ anyone. There's definitely something fishy about him."

"Well, it appears that the Montgomery family have some skeletons in their cupboard too."

"Yes, that's true. Listen. While you (7. finish) __________ what you're doing, I'll go through the diary. Maybe I can (8. find) __________ some sort of clue."

"That's a good idea James. Then afterwards we can go for lunch."

Chapter 7: A Suspect is Followed

Hudson settled down with the diary, only the click of Elvira's keyboard disturbing the silence.
He studied the entries in the diary, starting a week ago:

Friday:
Check blue chip shares of Kline Insurance.
Ring LW and confirm appointment.
Make table reservation for 8 pm at Sarco's.

Übung 53: Spiegelt der Satz den richtigen Sachverhalt wider? Markieren Sie mit richtig ✔ oder falsch – !

ÜBUNG 53 !

1. Jeremy Paxton is a very pleasant man. ☐
2. Sir Reginald is Hudson's boss. ☐
3. The Montgomerys employ servants. ☐
4. Hudson and Elliot are sharing an office. ☐
5. Sir Bernard is head of the IT department. ☐

Monday:
Ring SB and give progress report on analysis.
Buy security issues for Falcon.
Check price of Comtec.
Tuesday:
Dentist 2 pm.
Speak to JP about Hugh.
Buy steaks and salad for dinner.

"Ah," thought Hudson. "He disappeared some time on Wednesday."

Wednesday:
Fortnightly share transactions!
Speak to IT ref. new monitor.
7 pm meet PM at Rose & Crown.

! ÜBUNG 54

Übung 54: Unterstreichen Sie die richtige Alternative!

Hudson (1.) were/was unable to make sense of (2.) each/all the abbreviations. He suspected that the last entry for Wednesday evening (3.) could/can be significant.
"Elvira, any idea (4.) what/which PM could mean?"
"Prime Minister?"
"No. I (5.) doesn't/don't think Charlie was meeting the Prime Minister for a beer."
"What does the entry (6.) tell/say?"
"7 pm meet PM at Rose & Crown."
"It could mean anything, James. I've no idea."
"Oh well. I'll just (7.) make/do a photocopy of the page, then return

it to his office. Shall we do lunch when I'm back?"
"Yes, let's. My tummy is starting to rumble."

One minute later Hudson came rushing into the office.
"Elvira, quick. As I was taking the diary back to the office, I saw Jeremy Paxton acting very suspiciously. I think he's leaving the bank. Let's follow him."
"Okay. I'll just grab my coat and brolly."
They followed Paxton at a safe distance. He was walking very fast and occasionally turned round to see if he was being followed. Hudson thought they had lost him, but he saw the flash of Paxton's blue jacket enter the doors of a pub. They stopped on the corner, rather out of breath. Hudson, glancing up at the pub sign, received a shock.
Public House. Rose & Crown: Pub grub served all day.
"Elvira. This must be the same pub as in Charlie's diary. 7 pm, the Rose & Crown."
"But what about the initials, PM? Jeremy Paxton is JP."
"Maybe Greaves meant Paxton and Montgomery, PM?"

Übung 55: Welche Wörter haben eine ähnliche Bedeutung? Ordnen Sie zu!

1. last	☐ behave
2. tummy	☐ important
3. act	☐ go back
4. significant	☐ sometimes
5. return	☐ fast
6. occasionally	☐ stomach
7. quick	☐ final

ÜBUNG 55 !

"It's possible James, but didn't you tell me that they are on first name terms in the office?"
"That's right. It can't be helped. You'll have to go in there."
"Me! Why me?"
"Because Paxton knows me, but he's never seen you, as far as I know."
"That's true. Okay. Wish me luck."
"Good luck, Elvira. Oh, and be careful and don't take any risks."
"I will be careful, and I won't take any risks James. Stop being such a fusspot."
"Sorry. Off you go."
Elvira disappeared inside the pub and Hudson waited impatiently outside, hoping he had made the right decision.

! ÜBUNG 56

Übung 56: Übersetzen Sie!

1. shares ______________________
2. assets ______________________
3. investments ______________________
4. withdraw (money) ______________________
5. transfer slip ______________________
6. mortgage ______________________

Elvira Elliot entered the pub and went straight to the bar. She had a quick look around, but couldn't see Paxton anywhere.
"A tonic water please."
"Certainly Miss," replied the barmaid. "How about some pub grub?"

"No thanks. I thought I saw an old friend walk in just now. Jeremy Paxton. Do you know him?"
"Jerry? He's one of our regulars. He went into the snug bar a few minutes ago."
"Where's that?"
"It's through that door next to the toilets."
"Thanks."
"Don't mention it, dear."
Elvira grabbed her tonic water and wandered into the snug bar. Paxton was sitting in the corner, talking to an attractive, but hard-looking woman of about her own age. Elvira sat at the table next to theirs, picked up a menu from the tabletop and pretended to study it intensely. Elvira put her hand in her coat pocket to get a tissue. She felt something hard and plastic.
Then she smiled.
The two of them were whispering, but Elvira managed to catch snatches of their conversation.

Übung 57: Lesen Sie weiter. Übersetzen Sie die Wörter in Klammern und vervollständigen Sie den Text!

ÜBUNG 57 !

"Things are getting out of hand. I want out."

"You're in too (1. tief) ______________ Paxton. It's too late to get out now." "I only did it because of my (2. Schulden) ________________."

"Listen Paxton. We paid you a lot of money. Now you can clear all your debts."

"I want more money, (3. sonst) _______________ I'll go to the police."

"If you do, then you'll go to (4. Gefängnis) ____________________."

"I don't care. My nerves are all shot."

"Look. I'll speak to my people. I'm sure I can (5. überzeugen) ____________________ them to let you have more money. But you must promise that you'll make no more demands after that."

"I promise."

"Right. You'd better get back to work. Go now and I'll wait ten minutes before I leave."

While Paxton was putting his (6. Jacke) ____________________ on, Elvira finished her drink and left the pub. She ran to Inspector Hudson, who was pacing up and down on the corner.

"James! He'll be coming out any minute. Make sure he doesn't see you."

Hudson turned to face a shop window. He could see the front door of the pub in the (7. Spiegelung) ____________________.

"There he is now. Who did he meet?"
"Some woman. I didn't recognise her. She said that she would leave ten minutes after him. Right. He's gone now."
Hudson turned back to face her.
"Did you manage to listen in at all?"
"Yes."
Elvira reported the conversation to him.
"Ah, good. Now I think we're getting somewhere."

"James! Look! There she is." Hudson whirled round, just in time to see a woman, dressed in a raincoat, headscarf and sunglasses, disappearing into the crowd.

Übung 58: Bringen Sie die Wörter in die richtige Reihenfolge!

ÜBUNG 58 !

1. follow decided Paxton to Hudson

____

2. think somewhere now getting we're I

____

3. to went bar Elvira the straight

____

4. didn't the recognise woman she

____

5. conversation Elvira the reported Hudson to

____

6. left finished and pub she drink her the

____

Hudson grabbed Elvira's arm.
"Come on. Let's see if we can follow her."
They ran to where they had last seen the woman, but there was no sign of her.
"Blast," said Hudson panting. "We've lost her."
"Did you recognise her, James?"

"No. Not really. But somehow, she seems familiar."
"How do you mean?"
"The way she holds her head. I've seen her before, I'm sure."
"Well, Inspector," said Elvira ironically. "Today is your lucky day, if I'm not mistaken."

ÜBUNG 59 !

Übung 59: Bilden Sie Adverbien zu den vorgegebenen Adjektiven!

1. serious ______________________
2. quiet ______________________
3. bad ______________________
4. careful ______________________
5. quick ______________________
6. perfect ______________________

"What the devil are you taking about, Elvira?"
With that, she took something out of her pocket and waved it under Hudson's nose.
"What's that?"
"This, my dear James, is the Dictaphone that was lying on the desk. I meant to record the conversation at the Montgomerys' last night, but then I realised that I'd left my coat in the back of your car."
"And you were able to tape the whole conversation?"
"Yes, I did," chuckled Elvira with a self-satisfied smirk.
"Oh! You little beauty," shouted Hudson. He picked her up under the arms and swung her round in circles.
"James!" Elvira shrieked. "Put me down!"

Übung 60: Lesen Sie weiter und setzen Sie ein!
(background, complete, laboratory, pressed, whispering, volume, traffic, voice)

When they got back to the bank, they went to their office. Hudson rewound the tape and (1.) ________________ play.

There was a lot of interference from (2.) ________________ going past the window and also a lot of (3.) ________________ noise from the other guests in the pub.

"I can't really understand what they are saying, Elvira."

"Yes, they were (4.) ________________, trying not to be overheard. Turn it up a bit."

"No, that just makes the interference louder."

"Turn the (5.) ________________ down then and try listening with this headset."

"That's no good either. I've heard that woman's (6.) ____________ somewhere before, but the whispering has altered the tone slightly."

"Oh, dear. And I was so proud of myself."

"And you have a right to be, Elvira. Not to worry. I'll send the tape to the (7.) ________________ at the Yard. I'm sure that they can delete most of the traffic noise and interference."

"Good. I'll need about an hour to (8.) ________________ my database search."

"Go ahead. I need to make some phone calls."

Chapter 8: A Telephone Conversation with Mrs Greaves

Hudson placed a call to Scotland Yard and arranged for the tape to be collected by express courier. Then he telephoned Mrs Greaves.
"548 7122. Can I help you?"
"Is that Mrs Janet Greaves?"
"Yes it is. Who is this?"
"It's Inspector Hudson of Scotland Yard, Mrs Greaves."
"Oh! Have you found Charlie?"
"I'm afraid not, Mrs Greaves. All I can say is that we have a couple of very promising leads."
Mrs Greaves started to sob.
"Inspector. I'm so scared. I want my Charlie back."
"I know it's hard, Mrs Greaves. Look. If someone had kidnapped your husband for money, they would have demanded a ransom by now. I'm taking this as a sign that he's all right. I promise you that I will do my best to solve this crime as fast as possible and to get Charlie back for you, unharmed."
"Thank you, Inspector."

ÜBUNG 61 !

Übung 61: Übersetzen Sie!

1. Kann ich Ihnen helfen?

2. In welcher Branche sind Sie tätig?

3. Frau Greaves hat gerade ein Kind bekommen.

4. Ich werde mein Bestes tun diesen Fall zu lösen.

____

5. Charlie Greaves ist entführt worden.

____

6. Elvira hat das Gespräch auf dem Diktiergerät aufgenommen.

____

"It's the least I can do, Mrs Greaves. Now, I have a very delicate matter to discuss with you."
"What's that, Inspector?"
"Well, erm, I've received reports that there might be a possibility you're seeing someone else."
"I don't quite understand what you mean, Inspector?"
"To put it in plain English, Mrs Greaves, there is a rumour going around that you have a secret lover."
"Oh, poppycock, Inspector! I bet you got the information from Mr Harris, my silly next door neighbour. He's always poking his nose into other people's business."
"I'm sorry, Mrs Greaves. I'm not allowed to disclose my information sources."

Übung 62: Setzen Sie, wenn nötig, den fehlenden Artikel ein!

ÜBUNG 62 !

1. Mrs Greaves has ______ love affair.

2. Elvira is ______ insurance agent.

3. Miss Paddington often watches ______ television.

4. Hudson and Elliot had ______ lunch in the canteen.

5. Sir Bernard goes home after ______ work.

6. They went for dinner at ______ Montgomery Castle

"Well, I bet it was him. Wait till I see him. I'll..."
"Mrs Greaves. It's not important where I got the information. What is important is whether it is true or not?"
"It's not true, Inspector. I love Charlie very much."
"But this report said that a man has been seen entering your house, and then leaving a couple of hours later. Apparently, this has been happening two or three times per week?"
"It was Harris! I'll wring his neck!"
"Mrs Greaves, please!"
"Sorry Inspector. All I can say is that it's not true."
"So nobody has been coming to your house, two or three times a week, when your husband was working?"
"That part is true, Inspector, but it is definitely not my lover, I can assure you."

ÜBUNG 63 !

Übung 63: Setzen Sie die richtigen Präpositionen ein!

"I think you had better explain yourself, Mrs Greaves."

"The man is my brother Tony, Inspector."

"Why would your brother have (1.) ______ visit you secretly?"

"Because Charlie banned me (2.) ______ ever seeing him again."

"What (3.) ______ earth for?"

"Well, I'd rather not say, Inspector. It's just too embarrassing for me."

"Look Mrs Greaves. Some people are assuming that your husband ran (4.) ______ with the money, because he found out that you had a lover. If you can prove this wrong, then I can cross him off my list (5.) ______ suspects."

"Okay, Inspector. My brother has an alcohol and drug problem. We used (6.) ______ help him all the time and Charlie even paid for a therapy (7.) ______ a private clinic. Anyway, we visited him in the clinic. Afterwards his therapist told us that, once he was clean, we shouldn't help him any more. He said it would make it more difficult for Tony to stop, should he start again, if he knew that he could get food and money from us."

"And you've been giving him food and money?"

"Yes. I mean, he's my brother. I can't just ignore him when he's starving and broke. Charlie would go crazy, if he knew."

"Well, he won't hear it (8.) ______ me, Mrs Greaves. I'd like to thank you for your cooperation."

"Don't thank me, Inspector. Just bring my Charlie back safe and sound."

"I'll do my utmost, Mrs Greaves. Goodbye."

"Goodbye, Inspector."

Hudson hung up the phone, deep in thought.

"James?"

"Yes, Elvira?"

"I'm a little hungry, after having chased Paxton through the streets. I'll just nip to the canteen. Can I get you anything?"
"Could you get me a ham and cheese sandwich, Elvira?"
"Of course."
"Here, let me give you the money."
"My treat, James."
"Thanks very much."

ÜBUNG 64 !

Übung 64: Setzen Sie die Sätze ins Passiv!

1. Scotland Yard employs lots of people.

____

2. They followed Paxton to the pub.

____

3. Someone cleans Hudson's office every day.

____

4. Somebody has stolen the money.

____

5. Elvira likes Hudson.

____

When Elvira returned ten minutes later, she had a look of consternation on her face.
"What's wrong, Elvira?"
"I just witnessed the strangest thing, James."

"What?"
"As I went into the canteen, it was empty, apart from Sir Bernard and Paxton sitting alone in a corner."
"Nothing unusual about that, Elvira."
"True. But as I was entering, I saw Sir Bernard pass a rather bulky envelope to Paxton."
"What do you think was in it?"
"I would guess money, and judging by the thickness of the envelope, quite a lot of money."
"Hmm. Things appear to be coming to a head."
"Something tells me that you're right, James."

Übung 65: Sind die Sätze grammatikalisch korrekt? Markieren Sie mit richtig ✔ oder falsch – und verbessern Sie, wenn nötig!

1. Sir Bernard did give Paxton an envelope. ☐

____

2. Hudson has driven Elvira to the castle. ☐

____

3. Hudson was issued a new mobile phone. ☐

____

4. I am born in London. ☐

____

5. Hudson waited outside the pub. ☐

____

6. Elvira lives in the near of Hyde Park. ☐

Suddenly Hudson's mobile on the desk started humming and vibrating.
"I think you're receiving a text message, James."
"Oh dear."
"What is that supposed to mean?"
"Someone texted me a few days ago and I think I deleted it by mistake."
"Give it to me, I'll show you."
"What would I do without you, Elvira?"
"Look James. First you press the 'menu' button. Right?"
"Right."
"See that? It says, message received."
"Ah, yes."
"Now press the corresponding button."
"Now it says, read text, yes/no."
"Right, so press the yes button and you can read the text."
"Got it. Good. It's from the lab at the Scotland Yard. They say that they've managed to erase most of the background and traffic noise on the tape. Ah! This is good news. The courier will deliver it back to us in about an hour."
"Great."

ÜBUNG 66 !

Übung 66: Welche Sätze haben die gleiche Bedeutung? Ordnen Sie zu!

1. Give it to me.	☐ Let me pay.
2. What do you mean?	☐ The end is near.

3. Things are coming to a head. ☐ Pass it here.
4. It's my treat. ☐ What's up?
5. Don't thank me. ☐ Explain yourself!
6. How are you doing? ☐ My pleasure.

Deciding to confront Sir Bernard about what he gave to Paxton, Hudson told Elvira, "I'm going to see Sir Bernard."
"Right you are, James. I don't need too much longer now."

Hudson headed in the direction of the reception area and was puzzled that the bank appeared empty. When he arrived at reception, Ms Martorelli was typing on her word processor.
"Ms Martorelli, where is everybody?"
"They're all at the AGM, Inspector."
"I've always wondered what AGM stands for?"
"Annual General Meeting, Inspector. It's a shareholders' meeting that is held once a year."
"How long will it last for?"
"It's hard to say, Inspector. They've only just begun. Last year it went on for five hours."
"Right. Thank you very much."
"You're welcome."

Übung 67: Unterstreichen Sie die richtige Alternative!

ÜBUNG 67 !

Hudson returned (1.) at/to the office where Elvira was almost finished.
"Any (2.) luck/lucky, Elvira?"
"I'm afraid not. I'm just going through the last of the shares files."
"So all your (3.) works/work was for nothing?"

"I wouldn't say that, James. I've really learned a lot. I can (4.) too/also see why Charlie Greaves is so respected here."
"How can you see that?"
"(5.) Also/Well, all the investments he made. The man is a financial genius, but more importantly, he has (6.) a/an instinct when shares are going to (7.) get up/rise or fall. He's made the bank's clients, and also the bank, a lot of money."

"How does this shares thing work, Elvira?"
"You see James, shares, or stocks as they are called in America, are offered for sale, by companies, to the public. Companies normally use a bank to underwrite the issue. The bank then gets a fee and promise to purchase the security issue for a pre-arranged price on a certain day. Buying a share gives the purchaser part-ownership of the company. So they are entitled to vote at AGMs..."
"...and one of those is going on as we speak in the conference room," Hudson interrupted her explanations.
"Wow! The shareholders are entitled to a proportion of the distributed profits in the form of a dividend, so I don't think they are going to be happy about the missing 25 million."
"But surely the bank has insurance?"
"Let's hope so, James. Let's hope so."

ÜBUNG 68 !

Übung 68: Beantworten Sie die Fragen zum Text!

1. What kind of meeting is taking place at the moment?

____

2. What are shares called in America?

____

3. Why is Greaves so respected at the bank?

4. What does buying shares give the purchaser?

5. How long did the AGM go on for last year?

Chapter 9: Elvira is Attacked

Ten minutes later, Elvira got up from her desk.
"I've finished, James. Sorry for not finding anything."
"That's not your fault, Elvira. Thanks very much for a job well done."
"I need to go to the toilet. I'll be back in a jiffy."
"Should I make us some more coffee?"
"Sounds good to me, James."
Hudson made the coffee, took all the relevant documentation out of his briefcase and started to analyse it.
As he reached for his mobile to check if he had any messages, he knocked a pile of his paperwork to the floor.
Cursing, he knelt down and started picking the papers up. Suddenly, he noticed a piece of notepad paper that had somehow got stuck between two A4 sheets.
Turning it over, he said to himself, "that's where they got to. My notes from the board meeting."
He quickly scanned the notes. All of a sudden, a big schoolboy grin appeared on his face and he whispered, "Eureka!"

ÜBUNG 69 !

Übung 69: Ordnen Sie die folgenden Sätze zu einem sinnvollen Telefongespräch!

1. Could you ask him to call Hudson asap?
2. I'm sorry, he's out to lunch.
3. Thanks. Bye.
4. Could you put me through to Sir Reginald please?
5. Certainly.
6. Okay. I'll tell him.
7. Could you give him a message please?

Reihenfolge: _ _ _ _ _ _ _

Ten minutes later, Elvira still hadn't returned.
"Where can she be?" Hudson muttered to himself. "Surely powdering her nose can't take that long?"
Hudson waited another five minutes.
Now more worried than annoyed, Hudson made his way to the ladies toilet at the end of the corridor.
He put his fist up to knock, but then had second thoughts.
"What if Elvira isn't in there, but someone else is? I'll never get over the humiliation."
Instead of knocking, he put his ear to the door's surface.
There was utter silence.
Finally, he plucked up his courage and knocked on the door, whispering, "Elvira. Are you in there?"
No response.
Hudson was scared now, and he ran to reception as fast as he could.
"Ms Martorelli! Have you seen my colleague, Inspector Elliot?"
"I'm afraid not, Inspector. Just a moment. Yes. She came past here with some sandwiches about forty minutes ago."

"No. I mean since then?"
"Sorry, Inspector."
"She popped to the ladies about twenty minutes ago and she didn't come back."
"Well, maybe she's still in there?"

Übung 70: Welche Gegenteile gehören zusammen? Ordnen Sie zu!

ÜBUNG 70 !

1. courage	☐ law-abiding
2. whisper	☐ bent
3. clean	☐ cowardice
4. criminal	☐ release
5. straight	☐ shout
6. arrest	☐ dirty

Hudson coughed nervously.
"I went there before I came here. I knocked and called her name, but there was no reply."
"Oh, I see."
"Could you possibly check the toilet for me, Ms Martorelli?"
"I'm not really supposed to leave my desk, Inspector. But I could ask Sandra in Accounts to stand in for me, just for a few minutes."
"Thanks. I appreciate it."
"Don't mention it, Inspector. Sir Bernard said that we were to give you every possible assistance."
Hudson paced up and down like a tiger in its cage until Sandra arrived. Then they made straight for the toilets, with Ms Martorelli struggling to keep up.
She entered the ladies toilet, muttering something about paranoid men.

Hudson fidgeted outside, looking as though he needed the toilet badly himself.

Without warning, a piercing scream rendered the air.

Übung 71: Unterstreichen Sie die richtige Alternative!

1. Paxton lent/borrowed a lot of money.
2. The desktop seems to be lose/loose.
3. Hudson should have checked/controlled the plug.
4. Please bring/take this plate to the canteen.
5. Could you please hear/listen to me?

"Inspector! Help! Come quickly!"

Hudson barged the door open with his shoulder and, for the first time in his adult life, entered the ladies toilet.

Elvira Elliot was lying, unmoving, on the floor.

Ms Martorelli was starting to get hysterical.

"Inspector, I think she's dead. Oh my God!"

"Calm down, Ms Martorelli. Panic will not help the situation."

He knelt down next to Elvira and felt for a pulse.

"She's still alive. Now quickly, go and call an ambulance."

"Yes, Inspector."

Ms Martorelli ran for the door, sobbing all the way.

Übung 72: Lesen Sie weiter und setzen Sie die Wörter in der Klammer ein!

(attempted, terrible, tested, complete, fallen, unwrapped, struck)

Hudson (1.) ________________ Elvira's breathing, which was strong and steady. Her forehead was quite hot, so he (2.) ________________ some toilet paper, wet it, and mopped her brow.

Elvira's body gave a jerk and she (3.) ________________ to sit up.

"Ow! My head. James! What are you doing here? Get out. I must look (4.) ________________."

"It's all right, Elvira. An ambulance is on its way. You must have (5.) ________________ and knocked your head on the tiles."

"Oh, I didn't slip, James. I was attacked."

"Who by?"

"If only I knew. As I came out of the cubicle, I was jumped on and (6.) ________________ on the head with something very hard."

She put her fingers to her head and groaned.

"Let me have a look. Well, there's no blood, Elvira, but you've got a lump the size of an Easter Egg."

"It feels like a football to me."

Just then the paramedics arrived and gave Elvira a (7.)________________ examination.

When they had finished, Hudson asked, "What's the diagnosis?"
"A very mild concussion, sir. We gave her some aspirin, but she'll have a whopping headache for a day or two."
"What further treatment would you recommend?"
"Really just a couple of days taking it easy. Preferably in a dark-

ened room. If the headache isn't gone by the day after tomorrow, she should consult a doctor."

"Thanks very much. I owe you one."

Elvira, a snow-white bandage wrapped around her head, gave Hudson a smile.

"Thanks James. If you could leave me alone for a few minutes, I'd like to freshen up."

"Are you sure you'll be all right?"

"I'll be fine. Just give me a chance to make myself presentable."

"Okay. I'll wait for you outside."

ÜBUNG 73

Übung 73: Vervollständigen Sie die Fragen!

1. You can speak German, *can't you?*
2. Hudson doesn't like tea bags, ____________?
3. Elvira wasn't listening, ____________?
4. Don't drop the Dictaphone, ____________?
5. Hudson will get his man, ____________?
6. James drives a Bentley, ____________?

When Elvira exited the toilet a few minutes later, she was wearing a confused expression.

"What's the matter, Elvira?"

"I've been robbed, James."

"What? Has someone stolen your purse?"

"No. The Dictaphone. When we took the tape out, I hooked the Dictaphone onto my belt, then forgot all about it."

"But it's useless without a tape."

"We know there was no tape in it, James, but whoever attacked me obviously didn't. Anyway, we'll have the tape soon. Then we'll know who is guilty."
"I already know, Elvira."
"You know? James. Tell me. Tell me."
"Not yet Elvira. I need to make a phone call first. Then I should know for sure."
"James. Please?"
"You go to the canteen and get a cup of tea. I'll pick you up there in about ten minutes. That's a direct order."
"Oh, James! You're such a beast."

Übung 74: Bringen Sie die Wörter in die richtige Reihenfolge!

! ÜBUNG 74

1. for leave few me minutes alone a

____

2. a make first need I call to phone

____

3. at pick the reception up I'll you desk

____

4. you direct I'm a giving order

____

5. treatment would further recommend you what?

____

Hudson returned to his office and placed his phone call. Then he collected all his evidence, put it in his briefcase and left the office. As he was walking past reception, Ms Martorelli beckoned to him. "Hello! Inspector. There's a man here to see you. He said he needs to speak to you personally."

Hudson glanced over to the couch, where a very well-built man, dressed in black leather and wearing a crash helmet, was getting up.

His heart skipped a beat and he prepared to defend himself.

The man growled, "Inspector Hudson?"

"That's me," said Hudson, taking a step backwards.

"Scotland Yard courier, sir. I was instructed to only hand over this package to you in person."

Hudson breathed a sigh of relief.

Übung 75: Übersetzen Sie!

! ÜBUNG 75

1. Hudson hat sich Sorgen um Elvira gemacht.

2. Er ist noch nie in einem Schloss gewesen.

3. Der Mann in Leder sah sehr bedrohlich aus.

4. Er war zum ersten Mal in einer Damentoilette.

5. Sie hoffen, mehr Beweise zu finden.

"Ah! The tape. Thank you very much."
"My pleasure, sir."
It was only when the man turned to leave that Hudson saw the word 'Police' written in big white letters across the back of the leather jacket.
Thanking Ms Martorelli too, Hudson went to the canteen to collect Elvira.
She was sitting at a table, a steaming cup of tea in front of her. Her eyes were closed.
On hearing his footsteps, her eyes flew open.
"It hurts, James."
"I bet it does. Look, let me get you a taxi to take you home. I think you've had enough excitement for one day."
She gave Hudson a quizzical look.
"James. I thought you knew me better than that. I do half the work in solving a crime. And now, just before the 'grand finale', you want to send me home?"

Übung 76: Lesen Sie weiter und ergänzen Sie den Dialog mit den vorgegebenen Wörtern!
(lips, horses, paramedic, showdown, tomorrow, capitulated, taxi)

ÜBUNG 76

"The (1.) ________________ said you need rest, and peace and quiet."
"I can get that (2.) ________________, James. Wild (3.) ________________ will not get me out of this bank, until I know who did it."
"All right. So if I tell you who did it, will you then take a (4.) ________________ home?"

"No way."

"But you just said..."

"Watch my (5.) ________________, James. No!"

"But..."

"No buts, James. After working so hard, I want to be in at the final

(6.) ________________."

Hudson (7.) ________________.

"Okay Ms Elliot. Would you like to go to an AGM party?"

"Lead the way, kind sir."

Ms Martorelli was still manning the reception desk.
"Are you feeling better now, Ms Martorelli?"
"Much better, thank you, Inspector. Seeing your colleague lying on the floor gave me a big shock."
"Do you happen to have a tape recorder?"
"Actually, we do. We keep one for our French teacher, who comes in twice a week."
"Perfect. Could I borrow it, please?"
"Certainly, Inspector. Here you are."

ÜBUNG 77 !

Übung 77: Übersetzen Sie und enträtseln Sie das Lösungswort!

1. Diktiergerät _ _ _ _ _ _ _ _ _ ☐
2. Empfang _ _ _ _ _ _ _ _ ☐
3. Gepäck _ _ ☐ _ _ _ _
4. Handy _ _ _ _ ☐ _

5. Versicherung _ _ _ _ _ □ _ _ _
6. Überweisung _ _ _ □ _ _ _ _
7. Befehl _ _ □ _ _

Lösung: _ _ _ _ _ _ _ _

"Thank you. Now tell me. Where is the AGM being held?"
"Behind those double-doors over there, Inspector, but you can't go in."
"Why not?"
"Because it's a shareholders' meeting, by invitation only. As far as I know you are both neither shareholders, nor do you have an invitation."
"Ah, but that's where you're wrong, good lady. We do have an invitation."
"How can that be?"
"Here, I'll show it to you."
Hudson pulled out his wallet and extracted an identity card.

Übung 78: Welche ist die richtige Bedeutung der englischen Redewendungen? Kreuzen Sie an!

1. Hudson's feathers are ruffled.
   a) □ His clothes are untidy.
   b) □ He's getting annoyed.
   c) □ His hair is standing up.

2. It's raining cats and dogs.
   a) □ It's raining heavily.
   b) □ Things are falling from the sky.
   c) □ Rain is turning to snow.

3. He's tied up in a meeting.
   a) ☐ He's a prisoner.
   b) ☐ He's busy in a meeting.
   c) ☐ He's wrapping things up.

4. It's on the tip of her tongue.
   a) ☐ It tastes awful.
   b) ☐ She talks too much.
   c) ☐ She knows, but can't recall it.

"Here you are, Ms Martorelli."
"But that's your police ID card. It says, Inspector James Hudson, Scotland Yard, born on..."
Hudson snatched the card away.
"You don't look that old, Inspector."
"Yes. Let's skip that, shall we? This card entitles my colleague and me to enter that meeting."
"If you say so, Inspector."
Elvira pouted at Hudson.
"Can I have a look at the card, James?"
"No, you can't. Now let's go."

! ÜBUNG 79

Übung 79: Übersetzen Sie!

1. to participate ______________________

2. to investigate ______________________

3. to hesitate ______________________

4. to extract ______________________

5. to solve ______________________

6. to interrogate ______________________

"Now, Elvira. Before we go in: I want to keep a low profile, until a messenger arrives, who will hopefully confirm my suspicions."
"Whatever you say, James."
"Really, Elvira. Look, I know you can be very emotional and spontaneous, but please try and control yourself. I'd really appreciate it."
"I gave you my word, James."
"I know. It's just..."
"James. I hereby promise to be a good girl."
"That will be a first," muttered Hudson under his breath as they discreetly entered the conference room.

Übung 80: Lesen Sie weiter und unterstreichen Sie im Text die englische Übersetzung der Wörter in der Klammer!
(Aufruhr, Bericht, Leinwand, großzügig, verärgert, versichert, Diebstahl, Punkt)

The meeting was in turmoil. Consequently, nobody noticed Hudson and Elliot enter, then take a seat at the back.
The CFO was in the middle of his financial report. His presentation was in Powerpoint and a projector was projecting the images from his laptop onto a large screen at the back of the meeting room.
"As you can see, ladies and gentlemen, the last fiscal year was a very profitable one. We expect to be paying out a very generous dividend in a month or two."
Someone in the audience shouted. "What about the 25 million?"
The CFO became agitated.

"Yes, I know. We'll talk about that later. Now, if you could just let me finish my report."
Another voice called out. "What about next year's dividend? We want to know what's happened to all that money? Are we insured for theft?"
"Ladies and gentleman. Please! Sir Bernard will be addressing that issue, as soon as I have completed my report."

There was a big commotion in the room and people started to shout and even to boo. A couple of men were arguing very heatedly.
"It's okay for you."
"Why is it okay for me?"
"Because you're filthy rich anyway. I'm not rich and all my savings are invested in this silly bank."
"Well. That's not my fault, is it?"
"Oh! You rich people get on my nerves."
"And you poor people get on mine."
Hudson stepped across and spoke to them, before they could attack each other.
He sat down again shrugging his shoulders.
"They're just scared of losing all their money."
"So would I be, James."

Übung 81: Lesen Sie weiter und bringen Sie die Wörter in die richtige Reihenfolge!

(1. quietened a little down things.) ______________________

______________________ Suddenly, Elvira tugged at Hudson's sleeve.

"James, look!

(2. see woman sitting that do podium the you on?")

"Which one?"

"The younger one with the bleached blonde hair. That's the woman from the pub."

"Yes. I guessed as much. That's Penelope Montgomery."

(3. couldn't her Elvira excitement contain.)

"But James. Charlie's diary. He was meeting a PM at 7 pm in the Rose & Crown, the night he disappeared."

"That's right."

(4. "going, her aren't to you arrest well?")

"Not just yet, Elvira. We know that Paxton is probably involved, but I'm pretty sure there are others, too."

"See, James. She's noticed us. She seems awfully nervous, all of a sudden."
"Yes, she does."
"Watch out! She's leaving."
"Relax, Elvira."
"But James...?"
"She's left her handbag next to her chair. All she's got with her is her mobile. I don't know of a woman on this earth who would leave

her handbag, if she didn’t intend to come back.”
“Let’s hope you’re right, James.”
Hudson’s smile was confident, but inside, he wasn’t too certain.

Übung 82: Lesen Sie weiter und unterstreichen Sie die richtige Alternative!

The CFO continued (1.) saying/giving his financial report. Hudson noticed that all the board members were sitting together at the front. Hudson (2.) smiled/laughed when he saw that Dame Ethel Trowbridge had fallen asleep yet again.
“And that (3.) finishes/concludes the financial report for the last fiscal year. Any questions?”
“How (4.) many/much is the dividend going to be?”
“I would say in the region of two thousand five hundred pounds. Any (5.) more/nice questions?”
No further questions were forthcoming. Sir Bernard rose and (6.) shouted/whispered something in the CFO’s ear. Nodding in (7.) acknowledgement/detriment, he turned and faced the shareholders.
“Ladies and gentlemen. At this point, we will take a short break. Please be (8.) returned/back in your seats in fifteen minutes, then Sir Bernard Patterson, our vice chairman, will address the meeting. Refreshments are located in the foyer. Thank you.”

Übung 83: Sind die folgenden Aussagen korrekt? Markieren Sie mit richtig ✔ oder falsch – !

1. An investment banker sells insurance policies. ☐
2. Mr Harris doesn’t work in the bank. ☐

3. Penelope is Hugh Montgomery's sister. ☐
4. Hudson drives a Rolls Royce. ☐
5. Mr Burrows is head of accounts. ☐

On their way back to the meeting, they were walking through the foyer when they saw Jeremy Paxton. He was putting his coat on and walking towards the exit door.
Inspector Hudson called to him.
"Mr Paxton?"
"What do you want now, Inspector?"
"Please come back to the meeting. We have some things to discuss."
"I'm leaving, and you can't stop me."
"Maybe I can't, Mr Paxton. But those two extremely large policemen standing at the door can."
Paxton turned round cursing and returned to the meeting room.
Hudson and Elvira approached the two policemen at the door.
"Nobody gets out of here until I authorise it, okay?"
"Okay, Inspector."
Hudson put his mouth to the ear of one of the policemen and whispered something that Elvira didn't catch.

Übung 84: Lesen Sie weiter und setzen Sie die Wörter in der Klammer in die Lücken ein!
(complied, briefcase, prepared, important, audience, effect)

! ÜBUNG 84

They turned around and went back into the meeting room, where Sir Bernard Patterson was about to address the (1.) ____________ Hudson placed his (2.) ____________

and the tape recorder on the seat next to him and mentally (3.) ____________________ himself for what was coming.

Sir Bernard stepped up to the microphone.

"Ladies and gentlemen!"

This didn't have much (4.) ____________________ and the speculative murmur of voices continued.

"Order! Please. Ladies and gentlemen," shouted Sir Bernard.

This had the desired result and the room became quiet.

"Could everybody please switch off their mobile phones and laptops, before I begin."

There was chorus of 'beep, beep, beep', as most people (5.) ____________________ with the request.

Sir Bernard gave a sigh of frustrated anger as the door opened and the receptionist, Ms Martorelli, entered.

"What now, Ms Martorelli? This had better be (6.) ____________________."

"It's a very urgent note for Inspectors Hudson and Elliot, Sir Bernard. I'll just give it to them and leave again."

She handed the note to Hudson and left again as fast as she could.

Hudson read the note and smiled.

"Inspector Hudson? We haven't got all day, you know. May I proceed?"

Hudson stood up.

Chapter 10: Showdown at the AGM

"No, Sir Bernard. You may not."

A ripple of horrified shock went through the audience as Hudson made his way to the front, indicating to Elvira to follow him.

Elvira's eyes lit up like a child's on Christmas morning and she walked after him as fast as she could.

The palms of Hudson's hands were sweating.

Übung 85: Übersetzen Sie!

ÜBUNG 85

1. Could everyone please switch off your mobile phones?

____

2. He was walking towards the door.

____

3. Hudson read the note and smiled.

____

4. Sir Bernard stepped up to the microphone.

____

5. Hudson whispered something in the policeman's ear.

____

6. They turned around and went back into the room.

____

"Are you all right, James?"

"Yes. I'm fine, Elvira."
"It's just, you look rather pale and you're sweating."
"You see, I've never spoken in front of so many people."
"Look here, James! I've got my fingers crossed for you."
"Oh! Everything should be all right then."
With that, Hudson took a deep breath and stepped up to the microphone.

! ÜBUNG 86

Übung 86: Lesen Sie weiter und setzen Sie die richtigen Präpositionen ein!

"My Lords, ladies and gentlemen. Not all of you know me, so I would like (1.) ______ introduce myself."

There was complete silence (2.) ______ the room, except for a very soft snoring, emitting (3.) ______ Dame Ethel.

"My name is Inspector James Hudson (4.) ______ Scotland Yard."

A low rumble went through the crowd. As soon as Hudson started talking again, the silence returned.

"My colleague, temporary Inspector Elliot, and I were assigned to the case (5.) ______ the missing 25 million, but more importantly, the missing Mr Charlie Greaves, a key employee (6.) ______ this company."

Somebody called from the back.

"Have you found the money yet, Inspector?"

"Not yet. The money doesn't really interest me."

This caused a storm (7.) ______ protest.

"However!" Hudson said, speaking a little louder. "What does concern me is what happened to Mr Greaves, and why no ransom note was received. I interrupted this meeting in order to clear the matter up. As you are all, technically speaking, part-owners of the bank, I think you have a right to discover what went on."

People started to nod and peer forward with anticipation.

Hudson turned to face Sir Bernard.

"Sir Bernard. Could you step up to the microphone, please. I have a few questions that I would like to put to you."

Sir Bernard, apparently surprised, rose from his chair and approached Hudson.

"Just to confirm your identification, sir. You are Sir Bernard Patterson, Vice Chairman of the Warminster Bank?" he asked in an authoritative voice.

"Yes, I am."

"Sir Bernard. Were you involved in the kidnapping of Charles Greaves?"

"No, I wasn't."

Übung 87: Beantworten Sie die Fragen zum Text!

1. Who was snoring during the meeting?

____

2. What doesn't interest Inspector Hudson?

____

3. Why was Hudson nervous when he stepped up to the microphone?

---

4. Who brought the urgent note to Hudson?

---

5. Who asked Hudson, "May I proceed?"

"Did you participate in the stealing of approximately 25 million pounds?"

"No, I didn't. Is this some kind of joke, Inspector?"

"No, it isn't, Sir Bernard. I have one last question for you."

"Fire away."

"Did you give Jeremy Paxton an envelope, in the canteen, earlier today?"

"Yes."

"And what did the envelope contain?"

"Money. Two thousand pounds."

The crowd gasped.

"Was it a bribe of some sort, Sir Bernard?"

"No, Inspector. It was a loan."

"Could you explain please?"

"Jeremy Paxton came to see me a couple of days ago. He said that he had a small debt that he needed to clear up *asap*. He also informed me that he was expecting a significant inheritance within the next few weeks and would pay five hundred pounds interest back. I'm a banker, Inspector," Sir Bernard concluded, "I couldn't resist such a good deal."

Übung 88: Welche Wörter haben eine ähnliche Bedeutung? Tragen Sie die entsprechenden Ziffern ein!

ÜBUNG 88 !

1. loan	☐ sort
2. look	☐ important
3. participate	☐ credit
4. kind	☐ peer
5. show	☐ take part
6. significant	☐ demonstrate

"Can you confirm this, Mr Paxton?"
Paxton nodded his head and then looked at his shoes.
"Thank you very much, Sir Bernard. I just hope you can afford to lose two thousand pounds?"
Sir Bernard resumed his seat, but not before giving Paxton a very threatening look. The audience shifted restlessly. Hudson glanced at his notes.
"I would now like to call Mr Jeremy Paxton!"
Paxton's head snapped up from contemplating his shoes. He reluctantly made his way to the front. He had to pass within a couple of feet of Penelope Montgomery and as he did so, she whispered something that caused his eyes to widen in fear.

Übung 89: Stellen Sie die folgenden Fragen auf Englisch!

ÜBUNG 89 !

1. Sie möchten wissen, wo heute das AGM stattfindet.

Could you tell me where the AGM is taking place today?

2. Sie wollen wissen, ob Rauchen im Meeting erlaubt ist.

3. Sie fragen, wo es Erfrischungen gibt.

4. Sie fragen, ob die Gerüchte von dem gestohlenem Geld wahr sind.

5. Sie fragen, wie Sie Lord Montgomery anreden sollen.

"Mr Paxton. The same questions to you. Did you participate in stealing the 25 million pounds?"
"Yes, I did."
There was instant uproar in the audience.
"Quiet please," shouted Hudson. "Please let me carry on with my questioning."
Gradually, the tumult died down.
"Now then, Mr Paxton. Were you involved in the kidnapping of Charles Greaves?"
"Not directly. I told them I didn't want to get involved with kidnapping someone, but they made me do it. They threatened to tell the bank about all my gambling debts. If they had done, I would definitely have been sacked."
"That's no excuse, Mr Paxton. I hope you realise that you could go to prison for twenty to twenty-five years for these crimes."

ÜBUNG 90 !

Übung 90: Übersetzen Sie!

1. Hudson ist etwas nervös.

2. Elvira drückt ihm die Daumen.

---

3. Die Menge ist beunruhigt.

---

4. Paxton erwartet eine bedeutende Erbschaft.

---

5. Er wird wahrscheinlich ins Gefängnis müssen.

Hudson read fear in Paxton's eyes. He started to sob, then his eyes rolled upwards, as if looking for something in his brain, and he fainted!

Hudson managed to catch him before his head hit the floor and called out, "Is there a doctor in the house?"

An elderly man with white hair came to the front, saying, "I'm a doctor."

They carried Paxton to one side and the doctor began to examine him.

Now the crowd was really buzzing, as Hudson stepped back up to the microphone.

"I'd like to ask Lord and Lady Montgomery to join me."

The two aristocrats reluctantly walked forward.

"Thank you," said Hudson, bowing slightly despite himself.

"I have the same questions for you."

Lady Montgomery placed her hand on her husband's arm and said, "Let me deal with this, darling."

"All right, my love."

ÜBUNG 91 !

Übung 91: Setzen Sie die Wörter in der Klammer in die Lücken ein! ***(inheritance, disease, debts, involved, strength, crime, understand, specialist)***

"Inspector, we weren't (1.) ________________, but we knew what was going on. My husband has a terminal (2.) ________________. The only chance he has is to fly to the world's top (3.) ________________ in America. Of course, this would cost a lot of money, which we don't have."

"I don't (4.) ________________, Lady Montgomery. Surely 25 million is a bit much for such a specialist?"

"Yes, it is. Our family is up to its ears in (5.) ________________. We've been borrowing money, on the (6.) ________________ of our title, for years. It's got to the point where we'll never get out of debt and there will be no (7.) ________________ for our children."

"But you said you weren't involved. Did your daughter, Penelope, commit the (8.) ________________ on her own?"

All eyes turned to Penelope Montgomery, who was fuming with anger.

Lady Montgomery gasped.

"How did you know? Our children were only trying to take care of us."

"Children!" Hudson said, shocked.

Suddenly, there was a loud commotion in the audience, and Hugh

Montgomery could be seen running for the exit door, pushing people out of his way.
Elvira Elliot turned to Hudson.
"Quick, James. He's getting away. You could still cut him off, if you hurry."

Übung 92: Bringen Sie die Wörter in die richtige Reihenfolge!

1. participate the you did crime in?

______

2. confirm you that please can?

______

3. to would notes consult I like my

______

4. call now Paxton like I to would Jeremy

______

5. carry my questioning with me on let

______

6. been definitely would sacked have I

______

"Take it easy, Elvira. I think I have all possibilities covered."
Hudson watched in amusement as, a few seconds later, Hugh Montgomery threw open the exit doors. The two muscular policemen from earlier were blocking the exit, with their arms folded

across their chests. The larger of the two escorted the deflated Hugh Montgomery back to where Hudson was standing.
Hudson thanked him with a wink, then turned to the side.
"Ms Montgomery. Would you like to join us?" he asked the young woman.
Penelope Montgomery grabbed her handbag and stomped towards Hudson.
"You can't prove a thing. In Britain, people are innocent until proven guilty," she exclaimed.
The audience settled back, looking forward very much to the fun to come.
In the corner, Jeremy Paxton was slowly returning to consciousness.

Übung 93: Wie sagt man es auf höfliche Art und Weise? Kreuzen Sie an!

1. Sie fragen höflich, ob ein Stuhl frei ist.
   a) ☐ Can I have the chair?
   b) ☐ Is this chair taken?
   c) ☐ I really need this chair.

2. Sie bitten jemanden höflich um ein Taschentuch.
   a) ☐ Do you have a tissue?
   b) ☐ Have you got a tissue?
   c) ☐ May I have a tissue?

3. Sie fragen höflich, wo die Toiletten sind.
   a) ☐ Could you please direct me to the toilets?
   b) ☐ Can you tell me where the toilets are please?
   c) ☐ I need to see a man about a dog.

4. Ihr Kollege hat vor kurzem geheiratet. Was sagen Sie ihm?
   a) ☐ Good for you!
   b) ☐ My commiserations.
   c) ☐ Congratulations!

Hudson looked at Penelope Montgomery.
"If you think that I can't prove anything, Ms Montgomery, please listen to this tape."
He pressed the 'play' button and the conversation with Jeremy Paxton in the pub was played.
The audience listened attentively and Paxton nearly fainted again.
"That doesn't prove anything," Penelope said. "We could have been talking about anything."
"Ms Montgomery. Your family, especially your parents, seemed awfully keen to blame Charlie Greaves. They even invited us to dinner to inform us that his wife has a lover."
"Well, it's true," Hugh snarled. "I paid his neighbour, Mr Harris, five hundred quid for the information."
Hudson dialled a number on his mobile and ordered, "Bring her in."
A policeman escorted Janet Greaves into the meeting room.
"Mrs Greaves. Could you please tell us exactly what you told me on the phone, concerning not your lover, but your brother?"

Übung 94: Welches Wort ist das „schwarze Schaf"?

ÜBUNG 94 !

1. convict, criminal, suspect, warden
2. audience, spectators, participants, listeners
3. seatbelt, battery, radiator, fanbelt
4. cup, glass, mug, beaker
5. policeman, fireman, banker, soldier

She repeated her story and the Montgomery family looked crestfallen. Penelope Montgomery was still fighting for survival and said arrogantly, “Okay. So she doesn’t have a lover. It doesn’t mean that he didn’t steal the money.”
“That’s right,” said Hugh. “The last time I spoke to him, he was convinced that his wife was cheating on him. I bet he’s living it up in some sunny country right at this moment.”
“He isn’t,” said Hudson softly.
“How the heck would you know?” hissed Penelope.
Once again Hudson dialled a number on his mobile.
“Sir Reginald?”
Utter silence encompassed the whole room.
The doors opened and Sir Reginald walked in with Charlie Greaves!

ÜBUNG 95 !

Übung 95: Übersetzen Sie!

1. judge ____________________
2. lawyer ____________________
3. interest rates ____________________
4. exchange rate ____________________
5. unemployment ____________________
6. overdraft ____________________
7. standing order ____________________

Janet Greaves let out a scream and a sob and ran over and embraced him.

Penelope and Hugh Montgomery slumped their shoulders in resignation.

Hudson announced, "My Lords, ladies and gentlemen. May I introduce, Mr Charles Greaves."

The room was in uproar and the people that knew him went across and congratulated him. But Hudson wasn't finished yet.

"Order please. Order."

The people slowly took their seats again and quiet descended on the room.

"Mr Greaves. Could you please join us up here?"

Charlie Greaves made his way to the front, clutching his wife's hand.

Übung 96: Beantworten Sie die Fragen zum Text!

ÜBUNG 96 !

1. Who fainted and needed a doctor?

____

2. How did Hudson prove that Penelope was guilty?

____

3. Who tried to run from the meeting room?

____

4. Who did Hudson think was going to attack him?

____

5. Who threatened Paxton on his way to the front?

____

"Mr Greaves. I hope your ordeal wasn't too traumatic?" Hudson enquired.

"I'm just very dirty and very hungry, Inspector. Otherwise, I'm fine."

"I'm glad to hear it, Mr Greaves. Do you feel ready to tell us what happened?"

"Well. As you probably know, I was instructed by Sir Bernard to analyse all recent transactions. I discovered that they must have been made by a computer in our office. I automatically assumed that it was Jeremy, because of his gambling debts. Anyway, I confided in Hugh, who I thought was my friend. That afternoon I got a phone call from Penelope, saying that she badly needed my advice. She went on to say that she had a few thousand pounds to invest and whether I could meet her that evening for a drink in the pub."

ÜBUNG 97

Übung 97: Welche Zeitform ist richtig? Lesen Sie weiter und setzen Sie die richtige Verbform ein!

"What (1. happen) ________________ then?"

"We met, as (2. arrange) ______________. We (3. have) ______________ a couple of drinks and (4. speak) ________________ about investments for approximately one hour. Then she (5. ask) ______________ me if I could (6. drive) ________________ her to the train station."

"And did you do so?"

"It never got that far. All I remember is opening the passenger door for her, then I saw stars. I must have been hit on the head from behind."

Elvira nodded sympathetically.
"And where were you abducted to?"
"I woke up a few hours later in some stables. I now know that they were the Montgomery stables."
"Were you mistreated?"
"No. I was given bread and water. This morning they told me that they would let me go soon."
"Did you believe them?"
"I suppose so. They said that they would be flying to America with their parents in a few days and that they would leave instructions with the butler. He was to release me the day after they flew."
"Thank you, Mr Greaves."
Hudson turned to Penelope and Hugh.
"Where's the money?"
"I transferred it to different banks all over the world," said Hugh.
"Can you transfer it back?"
"I suppose so. I still have the authorisation code."
"Your penalty won't be so harsh if you do, Mr Montgomery. One more question."
"Yes?"

Übung 98: Unterstreichen und korrigieren Sie die „falschen Freunde"!

ÜBUNG 98 !

1. Hudson's chief is Sir Reginald.

____

2. In London, it's cheaper to stay in a pension.

____

3. This is the actual issue of *The Times*.

4. Elvira's brutto wages are quite high.

5. The bank is just a money-making fabric.

6. The amount of money stolen was very gross.

7. This appointment passes me very well.

"Well, we know now that the transactions were made from Mr Greaves's computer. How did you do it?" asked Hudson directly.

"That was easy. Charlie was always forgetting his password, so I suggested he use something simple, something he could easily remember."

Charlie Greaves nodded, "I remember."

"Well," Hugh Montgomery continued, "knowing Charlie quite well, I tried all the obvious combinations, but nothing seemed to work. It was rather frustrating. My last hope was his wife's birth date, so I rang personnel and told them that I wanted to send Mrs Greaves some flowers for her birthday. Luckily it's in a couple of weeks, so they didn't become suspicious. Anyway, I entered the number, and bingo!" he finished his explanations.

Übung 99: Vervollständigen Sie die Sätze!

1. For this case, Hudson and Elliot formed a ____________________.
2. People facing each other in a final confrontation is known as a ____________________.
3. The bank was founded or ____________________ in 1853.
4. Someone who might have committed a crime is a ____________________.
5. If your boss signs something which gives you permission to do something, it's an ____________________.
6. Money paid to a bank employee at the end of each month is a ____________________.

Hudson nodded, satisfied.
"Penelope Montgomery, Hugh Montgomery and Jeremy Paxton. I'm arresting you in the name of the law. You will be charged with grand theft, kidnapping with bodily harm and assaulting a police officer..."
"Just a minute," shouted Jeremy Paxton. "Penelope assaulted your colleague. I was walking past your office when I heard you playing the tape from the pub. I phoned her, to warn her straight away, but she was already here for the meeting... ."
Penelope Montgomery hit him on the shoulders with her handbag, saying, "Shut up, you idiot."
Hudson had heard and seen enough.
"Take them to the station, constable. Hold them until I arrive to place charges."

The three prisoners were led away.
Hudson then turned to Lord and Lady Montgomery.
"I'm not sure yet if you will be charged. You had knowledge of a crime and you didn't report it. I will have to consult with my superiors, then I will let you know the outcome."

ÜBUNG 100

Übung 100: Beantworten Sie die Fragen zum Text!

1. Where was Charlie Greaves kept prisoner?

____

2. Whose birth date was Charlie's password?

____

3. Who found Elvira unconscious in the toilets?

____

4. Who is Mrs Greaves' assumed lover?

____

5. Who overheard Hudson and Elliot playing the tape?

____

6. Why does Lord Montgomery need to go to America?

____

Hudson stepped up to the microphone again one last time.
"My Lords, ladies and gentlemen. I would like to apologise once more for the interruption, and thank you for your patience."

Sir Bernard started to clap. Slowly but surely, other people started to follow suit. The applause increased until Hudson held up his hands, gesturing for them to stop. The noise abated a little and Hudson bent to the microphone.
"Thank you. Thank you. It just wouldn't be right for me to take all the credit. I would never have been able to solve this crime, if it hadn't have been for the dedication and self-sacrifice of my colleague, acting Inspector Elvira Elliot!"
He waved Elvira to him. She turned as red as a beetroot and joined him at the front.
The applause started up once again, but this time a few of the men started stamping their feet as well.
Tears started streaming down Elvira's cheeks and all she could manage was a croaked, "James, you beast."
The microphone transmitted her words and the applause and stomping became like thunder.
Dame Ethel awoke with a start, and said, "Well, have the tea and biscuits arrived then?"

THE END

Abschlusstest

Übung 1: Welche Wörter gehören in die Lücken?
(favourite, Lords, sharp, member, transmitted, investment, dividend)

1. The microphone ______________________ her words.

2. My ______________________, ladies and gentlemen.

3. Charlie Greaves is an ______________________ officer for the bank.

4. Dame Ethel is a ______________________ of the board.

5. Hudson's ______________________ meal is shepherds pie.

6. At the end of the fiscal year, the shareholders receive a ______________________.

7. Lady Montgomery eats dinner at eight ______________________.

Übung 2: Unterstreichen Sie die richtige Alternative!

1. She has been waiting for Hudson for/since half an hour.
2. I'm afraid he's popped out of the office for a jimmy/moment.
3. They don't have very much/many time to solve the case.
4. Hudson would now like to drink a litre/pint of beer.
5. They walked down the gangway/corridor to reception.
6. The courier brought/took the tape to the bank.
7. Elvira was lying/laying unconscious on the floor.

Übung 3: Bringen Sie die Wörter in die richtige Reihenfolge!

1. his home Bentley drove in Hudson.

____

2. more interview to need people I

____

3. at weren't meeting why you the?

____

4. through just browse I'll files the

____

5. the taped Elvira conversation whole

____

6. understand mean don't what quite you I

____

Übung 4: Finden Sie die passende Übersetzung!

1. He regretted doing it.	☐ Sie beschuldigten mich.
2. They accused me.	☐ Er stellte ihnen Fragen.
3. He asked them questions.	☐ Sie gab zu, schuldig zu sein.
4. I must be going.	☐ Er bereute es getan zu haben.
5. See you later.	☐ Ich muss jetzt gehen.
6. She admitted her guilt.	☐ Bis später.

Übung 5: Beantworten Sie die Fragen zum Text!

1. Where did Hudson park at the bank?

2. Why wasn't Hugh Montgomery at dinner in the castle?

3. What is the surname of the entrepreneur?

4. Who is always asking for tea and biscuits?

5. Who gave money to Paxton in the canteen?

6. Whose conversation did Elvira listen to in the pub?

Übung 6: Bringen Sie die Sätze des Verhörgesprächs in eine sinnvolle Reihenfolge!

1. Can anyone confirm that?
2. That's right.
3. Thank you, Mr Paxton.
4. Where were you at 8pm last Wednesday?
5. Your name is Jeremy Paxton?
6. I was at home watching television.

7. Yes, my mother rang at five past eight.

Reihenfolge: _ _ _ _ _ _ _

Übung 7: Welche Sätze haben die gleiche Bedeutung? Ordnen Sie zu!

1. I'll have to speak to her.	☐ I'll wrap it up afterwards.
2. I'll tell him you've arrived.	☐ I'll be with you in a second.
3. I'll finish it later.	☐ I'll call the meeting off.
4. I'll be there in a minute.	☐ I must talk with her.
5. I'll be going now.	☐ I'll let him know you're here.
6. I'll cancel the meeting.	☐ I'm off.

Übung 8: Korrigieren Sie die Sätze!

1. Hudson and Elliot will have celebrated tonight.

____

2. Hudson has never gone to France.

____

3. Charlie Greaves had been kidnapped last week.

____

4. What time does the banks close?

____

5. Elvira does drive her car every day.

6. Paxton doesn’t likes anyone he meets.

7. I didn’t ever go to jail, up to now.

Übung 9: Übersetzen Sie!

1. Mein Handy funktioniert momentan nicht.

2. Hudson und Elliot wurden gestern zum Essen eingeladen.

3. Sir Bernard geht für gewöhnlich sehr schnell.

4. Die Montgomerys haben ein Schloss auf dem Land.

5. Deutschland hat 80 Millionen Einwohner.

6. Bevor er nach London zog, wohnte er in Bristol.

Übung 10: Was bedeuten die Redewendungen? Kreuzen Sie an!

1. Elliot was hot on Paxton's heels.
   a) ☐ Sie ist ihm in geringem Abstand gefolgt.
   b) ☐ Sie lief sehr nah neben ihm her.

2. Don't lay a finger on Elvira Elliot.
   a) ☐ Belästige Elvira Elliot nicht.
   b) ☐ Berühre Elvira Elliot nicht.

3. Inspector Hudson is the salt of the earth.
   a) ☐ Er ist sehr bodenständig.
   b) ☐ Er ist sehr zuverlässig und ehrlich.

4. Elvira tried not to let Hudson down.
   a) ☐ Sie wollte ihn nicht ärgern.
   b) ☐ Sie wollte ihn nicht enttäuschen.

5. Hudson likes to take 40 winks in his armchair.
   a) ☐ Er hält gern ein Schläfchen.
   b) ☐ Er liest und entspannt sich gern im Sessel.

6. Paxton is afraid that he will get the boot.
   a) ☐ Er hat Angst, dass er gefeuert wird.
   b) ☐ Er hat Angst, dass seine Kollegen zutreten werden.

Übung 11: Bringen Sie die Wörter in die richtige Reihenfolge!

1. confirmation please the me send order

....

2. record bookkeepers purchases all

3. mail is cheque in your the

4. invoice soon pay please possible as your as

Übung 12: Sind die Sätze grammatikalisch korrekt? Markieren Sie mit richtig ✔ oder falsch – und schreiben Sie, wenn nötig, die Sätze richtig auf!

1. Hudson likes not tea. ☐

2. Hudson works as a police inspector. ☐

3. Jeremy Paxton don't like anyone. ☐

4. Hudson is visiting Mrs Greaves tonight. ☐

5. What means tea-lady? ☐

6. Miss Evans has been with the bank since 45 years. ☐

Übung 13: Was bedeuten die englischen Redewendungen? Kreuzen Sie die richtige Lösung an!

1. Hudson has friends in high places.
   - a) ☐ He has friends living on a mountain.
   - b) ☐ He has friends with a lot of influence.
   - c) ☐ He has friends in a skyscraper.

2. Elvira doesn't miss much.
   - a) ☐ She isn't married.
   - b) ☐ She's a crack shot.
   - c) ☐ She's very aware of what is happening.

3. Hudson might be on a wild goose chase.
   - a) ☐ He is looking for Christmas dinner.
   - b) ☐ He is chasing criminals.
   - c) ☐ He is on a fruitless search.

4. Hudson always goes by the board.
   - a) ☐ He passes the meeting room.
   - b) ☐ He follows rules and regulations.
   - c) ☐ He ignores rules and regulations.

Übung 14: Setzen Sie die Sätze ins Present Perfect!

1. Hudson interviewed Hugh Montgomery.

....

2. Somebody attacked Elvira.

....

3. Your invoice was paid.

____

4. They found Elvira on the lying floor.

____

5. I didn't find my mobile phone.

____

6. Elvira never had caviar.

____

Übung 15: Welche Synonyme gehören zusammen? Setzen Sie die richtige Ziffer ein!

1. finish	☐ apprehend
2. noticed	☐ helpful
3. polite	☐ end
4. speech	☐ face
5. arrest	☐ saw
6. confront	☐ talk

Lösungen

Übung 1: 1. diary 2. stapler 3. filing cabinet 4. hole punch 5. rubber 6. ruler 7. calculator 8. sellotape
Übung 2: 1. nil 2. love 3. oh 4. nought 5. zero
Übung 3: 1. Please give me your mobile phone number. 2. Don't forget to dial the area code. 3. I'll text you tomorrow. 4. The battery has to be charged every few days. 5. I can't receive a strong signal in the cellar.
Übung 4: 1. Please take a seat. 2. I'm afraid we have a slight problem. 3. The report was due today. 4. I'll arrange an appointment with him. 5. He didn't show up for work this morning. 6. I'll get onto it right away.
Übung 5: 1. a 2. b 3. b 4. a 5. c
Übung 6: 1. on 2. for 3. that 4. this 5. for 6. in
Übung 7: 1. c 2. b 3. b 4. a
Übung 8: 1. catch 2. lamp 3. write 4. money 5. shorts 6. software
Übung 9: 1. minutes 2. attend 3. vote 4. introduce 5. chairman 6. performance 7. goal Lösung: meeting
Übung 10: 1. employees 2. somebody 3. arrogantly 4. capable 5. assured 6. cooperate
Übung 11: 1. lowered 2. stormy 3. first 4. innocent 5. nobody
Übung 12: 1. b 2. a 3. b 4. c
Übung 13: 1. The bank has 69 employees. 2. Hudson and Sir Bernard visit the IT department first. 3. The name of Inspector Hudson's boss is Sir Reginald. 4. Lord Montgomery is chairing the emergency meeting.
Übung 14: 1. accounting 2. pleasure 3. department 4. really 5. invoices 6. complicated 7. Inspector 8. profits
Übung 15: 1. made 2. come 3. related 4. met 5. replied 6. stopped
Übung 16: 1. (provision) commission 2. (actual) current 3. (proves) checks 4. (become) have/get 5. (sensible) sensitive 6. (personal) personnel 7. (spends) donates 8. (the gymnasium) grammar school
Übung 17: Reihenfolge: 3, 1, 5, 2, 4
Übung 18: 1. Miss Paddington is standing in the kitchen and cooking. 2. Hudson loves his old Bentley. 3. Hudson and Miss Paddington are expecting a visitor. 4. Somebody tipped off the newspaper. 5. Miss Paddington has never been abroad. 6. Elvira Elliot wants to talk to Inspector Hudson.
Übung 19: 1. silence 2. stated, remarked 3. give me 4. dessert, pudding 5. additional 6. fetch it 7. quickly 8. begin
Übung 20: 1. insurance agent 2. bank clerk 3. foreign currency 4. police officer 5. sales representative 6. exchange rate 7. order confirmation
Übung 21: 1. einen Fall zu Ende bringen 2. im Handschuhfach 3. Wir scheinen uns verfahren zu haben. 4. Fahren Sie am Kreisverkehr rechts. 5. Die Polizei zahlt sehr wenig. 6. ein paar wohlverdiente freie Tage

Übung 22: 1. immediate 2. save 3. beautiful 4. dear 5. wages 6. carefully 7. allowed

Übung 23: 1. Mrs Greaves will be questioned by Hudson later. 2. Mrs Greaves is visited regularly by someone. 3. Charlie Greaves has been kidnapped. 4. Elvira is being spoken to by Hudson at the moment. 5. Hudson was given the information by her. 6. Paxton doesn't like being told what to do by other people.

Übung 24: 1. on 2. in 3. on 4. in 5. out 6. in

Übung 25: 1. information 2. arrest 3. withholding 4. evidence 5. tough 6. notebook 7. jiffy 8. questioning

Übung 26: 1. much 2. many 3. much 4. many 5. much 6. many

Übung 27: 1. of 2. with 3. to 4. in 5. of 6. up 7. for

Übung 28: 1. He said Elvira was an insurance agent. 2. He said she was the best document investigator he knew. 3. She said that it sounded like a good idea. 4. He said that she wouldn't regret it. 5. She said that she hoped not.

Übung 29: 1. When can I start work? 2. How long will your investigation last? 3. Have you already spoken to Mrs Greaves? 4. Do you have five minutes for me? 5. What is your favourite kind of tea?

Übung 30: 1. investment officer 2. receptionist 3. bookkeeper 4. taxi driver 5. housekeeper 6. secretary

Übung 31: 1. printer 2. scanner 3. facsimile machine 4. computer terminal 5. intranet 6. access 7. files 8. password 9. entry

Übung 32: 1. We need a password to gain entry. 2. Hudson makes coffee while Elvira is getting the chair. 3. The office has everything they need. 4. Elvira would like to drink a cappuccino. 5. James forgot to plug in the coffee machine. 6. They will get access to the intranet.

Übung 33: 1. breakfast 2. password 3. electronic 4. computer 5. paperwork 6. preparing 7. seems 8. produced

Übung 34: 1. What if Hudson caught the guilty party? 2. What if you made the coffee? 3. What if the bank employees knew Elvira is an insurance agent? 4. What if Charlie Greaves were/was the thief? 5. What if Hudson couldn't solve a case? 6. What if you did all these exercises?

Übung 35: 1. looking 2. starting 3. Glancing 4. thanking 5. remembering 6. waiting 7. eating

Übung 36: 1. department 2. reward 3. schoolgirl 4. files 5. containing 6. beginning 7. relevant 8. something

Übung 37: 1. worker 2. bookshelf 3. floppy disk 4. Dictaphone 5. owe 6. car

Übung 38: 1. - (They were speaking about the transactions.) 2. ✔ 3. ✔ 4. - (Hudson visited Mrs Greaves yesterday.) 5. - (Elvira is working on the database now.) 6. ✔

Übung 39: 1. They are invited to dinner. 2. He grabbed his overcoat and briefcase. 3. We mustn't be late for dinner. 4. Lord Montgomery was chairing the meeting. 5. Hudson decided to take the stairs. 6. Elvira went shopping an hour ago.

Übung 40: Reihenfolge: 4, 2, 6, 1, 5, 3
Übung 41: 1. going to 2. illuminated 3. noticed 4. fortune 5. look at 6. told
Übung 42: 1. Hudson took Elvira to Montgomery Castle. 2. The butler has done his duty. 3. On the way to the castle, they stopped for petrol. 4. Elvira is looking very elegant tonight. 5. It cost Hudson a lot of money to fill up his car. 6. Elvira was getting very angry.
Übung 43: 1. politely 2. concerning 3. surprised 4. handle 5. conclusion 6. rumours 7. conclusive 8. convinced
Übung 44: 1. Lady Montgomery is not very nice. 2. Hudson doesn't feel very comfortable in the castle. 3. Elvira is slowly getting angry. 4. The dining room is bigger than Elvira's flat. 5. Lady Montgomery is trying to influence Hudson.
Übung 45: 1. left 2. true 3. pulled out 4. arrived at 5. inform
Übung 46: 1. up 2. in 3. to 4. from 5. at 6. of 7. in
Übung 47: 1. Miss Paddington gave sandwiches to Hudson. 2. Elvira had good and bad news for Hudson. 3. They have lunch in the canteen. 4. He hadn't got his number. 5. Jeremy Paxton acts as though he is hiding something.
Übung 48: 1. investigation 2. invitation 3. investment 4. files 5. pregnant 6. research
Übung 49: 1. b 2. a 3. b 4. b
Übung 50: 1. department head 2. Chairman of the Board 3. minutes 4. receptionist 5. Dictaphone
Übung 51: 1. How many people work as investment officers? 2. Have Hudson and Elliot teamed up? 3. Does it ever rain in London? 4. What is Hudson's favourite tea? 5. Who is head of the accounts department?
Übung 52: 1. went 2. shared 3. told 4. had 5. like 6. likes 7. finish 8. find
Übung 53: 1. - 2. ✔ 3. ✔ 4. ✔ 5. -
Übung 54: 1. was 2. all 3. could 4. what 5. don't 6. say 7. make
Übung 55: 1. final 2. stomach 3. behave 4. important 5. go back 6. sometimes 7. fast
Übung 56: 1. Aktien 2. Vermögen 3. Anlagen 4. (Geld) abheben 5. Überweisungsschein 6. Hypothek
Übung 57: 1. deep 2. debts 3. otherwise 4. prison 5. convince 6. jacket 7. reflection
Übung 58: 1. Hudson decided to follow Paxton. 2. Now I think we're getting somewhere. 3. Elvira went straight to the bar. 4. She didn't recognise the woman. 5. Elvira reported the conversation to Hudson. 6. She finished her drink and left the pub.
Übung 59: 1. seriously 2. quietly 3. badly 4. carefully 5. quickly 6. perfectly
Übung 60: 1. pressed 2. traffic 3. background 4. whispering 5. volume 6. voice 7. laboratory 8. complete
Übung 61: 1. Can I help you? 2. What branch are you in? 3. Mrs Greaves has had a baby. 4. I will do my best to solve this case. 5. Charlie Greaves has been kidnapped. 6. Elvira recorded the conversation on the Dictaphone.

Übung 62: 1. a 2. an 3. - 4. - 5. - 6. -
Übung 63: 1. to 2. from 3. on 4. off 5. of 6. to 7. in 8. from
Übung 64: 1. Lots of people are employed by Scotland Yard. 2. Paxton was followed to the pub by them. 3. Hudson's office is cleaned every day. 4. The money has been stolen. 5. Hudson is liked by Elvira.
Übung 65: 1. - (Sir Bernard gave Paxton an envelope.) 2. - (Hudson drove Elvira to the castle.) 3. ✔ 4. - (I was born in London.) 5. ✔ 6. - (Elvira lives near Hyde Park.)
Übung 66: 1. Pass it here. 2. Explain yourself! 3. The end is near. 4. Let me pay. 5. My pleasure. 6. What's up?
Übung 67: 1. to 2. luck 3. work 4. also 5. Well 6. an 7. rise
Übung 68: 1. An AGM is taking place at the moment. 2. They are called stocks. 3. He has an instinct for shares. 4. Buying shares gives the purchaser part-ownership of the company. 5. Last year the AGM went on for five hours.
Übung 69: Reihenfolge: 4, 2, 7, 5, 1, 6, 3
Übung 70: 1. cowardice 2. shout 3. dirty 4. law-abiding 5. bent 6. release
Übung 71: 1. borrowed 2. loose 3. checked 4. take 5. listen
Übung 72: 1. tested 2. unwrapped 3. attempted 4. terrible 5. fallen 6. struck 7. complete
Übung 73: 1. can't you? 2. does he? 3. was she? 4. will you? 5. won't he? 6. doesn't he?
Übung 74: 1. Leave me alone for a few minutes. 2. I need to make a phone call first. 3. I'll pick you up at the reception desk. 4. I'm giving you a direct order. 5. What further treatment would you recommend?
Übung 75: 1. Hudson was worried about Elvira. 2. He has never been in a castle. 3. The man in leather looked very threatening. 4. He was in a ladies toilet for the first time. 5. They are hoping to find more evidence.
Übung 76: 1. paramedic 2. tomorrow 3. horses 4. taxi 5. lips 6. showdown 7. capitulated
Übung 77: 1. Dictaphone 2. reception 3. luggage 4. mobile 5. insurance 6. transfer 7. order Lösung = England
Übung 78: 1. b 2. a 3. b 4. c
Übung 79: 1. teilnehmen 2. ermitteln 3. zögern 4. herausziehen 5. lösen 6. verhören
Übung 80: 1. turmoil 2. report 3. screen 4. generous 5. agitated 6. insured 7. theft 8. issue
Übung 81: 1. Things quietened down a little. 2. Do you see that woman sitting on the podium? 3. Elvira couldn't contain her excitement. 4. Well, aren't you going to arrest her?
Übung 82: 1. giving 2. smiled 3. concludes 4. much 5. more 6. whispered 7. acknowledgement 8. back
Übung 83: 1. - 2. ✔ 3. ✔ 4. - 5. -

Übung 84: 1. audience 2. briefcase 3. prepared 4. effect 5. complied 6. important
Übung 85: 1. Könnten bitte alle ihre Handys ausschalten? 2. Er lief gerade Richtung Tür. 3. Hudson las den Zettel und lächelte. 4. Sir Bernard machte einen Schritt auf das Mikrofon zu. 5. Hudson flüsterte dem Polizisten etwas ins Ohr. 6. Sie drehten sich um und gingen zurück ins Zimmer.
Übung 86: 1. to 2. in 3. from 4. of 5. of 6. in 7. of
Übung 87: 1. Dame Ethel was snoring during the meeting. 2. The money doesn't interest him. 3. He'd never spoken to so many people before. 4. Ms Martorelli brought the note. 5. Sir Bernard asked "May I proceed?"
Übung 88: 1. credit 2. peer 3. take part 4. sort 5. demonstrate 6. important
Übung 89: 1. Could you tell me where the AGM is taking place today? 2. Could you tell me if smoking is permitted in the meeting? 3. Could you tell me where the refreshments are? 4. Are the rumours about the stolen money true? 5. How do I address Lord Montgomery?
Übung 90: 1. Hudson is a little nervous. 2. Elvira is crossing her fingers for him. 3. The crowd is worried. 4. Paxton is expecting a significant inheritance. 5. He will probably have to go to prison.
Übung 91: 1. involved 2. disease 3. specialist 4. understand 5. debts 6. strength 7. inheritance 8. crime
Übung 92: 1. Did you participate in the crime? 2. Can you please confirm that? 3. I would like to consult my notes 4. I would now like to call Jeremy Paxton. 5. Let me carry on with my questioning. 6. I would definitely have been sacked.
Übung 93: 1. b 2. c 3. a 4 c
Übung 94: 1. warden 2. participants 3. seatbelt 4. glass 5. banker
Übung 95: 1. Richter 2. Rechtsanwalt 3. Zinssätze 4. Wechselkurs 5. Arbeitslosigkeit 6. Überziehungskredit 7. Dauerauftrag
Übung 96: 1. Jeremy Paxton fainted and needed a doctor. 2. Hudson played the tape to prove that Penelope was guilty. 3. Hugh Montgomery tried to run from the meeting room. 4. He thought the courier was going to attack him. 5. Penelope Montgomery threatened Paxton on his way to the front.
Übung 97: 1. happened 2. arranged 3. had 4. spoke 5. asked 6. drive
Übung 98: 1. (chief) boss 2. (pension) bed and breakfast 3. (actual) current 4. (brutto) gross 5. (fabric) factory 6. (gross) large/big 7. (passes) suits
Übung 99: 1. partnership 2. showdown 3. established 4. suspect 5. authorisation 6. salary
Übung 100: 1. Charlie was kept prisoner in the Montgomerys' stables. 2. Janet Greaves' birth date was Charlie's password. 3. Ms Martorelli found Elvira unconscious in the toilets. 4. Mrs Greaves' assumed lover is Tony, her brother. 5. Paxton overheard them playing the tape. 6. He needs to go to America to see a specialist.

Lösungen Abschlusstest

Übung 1: 1. transmitted 2. Lords 3. investment 4. member 5. favourite 6. dividend 7. sharp
Übung 2: 1. for 2. moment 3. much 4. pint 5. corridor 6. brought 7. lying
Übung 3: 1. Hudson drove home in his Bentley. 2. I need to interview more people. 3. Why weren't you at the meeting? 4. I'll just browse through the files. 5. Elvira taped the whole conversation. 6. I don't quite understand what you mean.
Übung 4: 1. Er bereute es getan zu haben. 2. Sie beschuldigten mich. 3. Er stellte ihnen Fragen. 4. Ich muss jetzt gehen. 5. Bis später. 6. Sie gab zu, schuldig zu sein.
Übung 5: 1. Hudson parked in the underground garage. 2. He said that his mare went into labour. 3. The entrepreneur's surname is Broadbent. 4. Dame Ethel is always asking for tea and biscuits. 5. Sir Bernard gave money to Paxton. 6. Elvira listened to Jeremy Paxton's and Penelope Montgomery's conversation in the pub.
Übung 6: Reihenfolge: 5, 2, 4, 6, 1, 7, 3
Übung 7: 1. I must talk with her. 2. I'll let him know you're here. 3. I'll wrap it up afterwards. 4. I'll be with you in a second. 5. I'm off. 6. I'll call the meeting off.
Übung 8: 1. Hudson and Elliot will celebrate tonight. 2. Hudson has never been to France. 3. Charlie Greaves was kidnapped last week. 4. What time do the banks close? 5. Elvira drives her car every day. 6. Paxton doesn't like anyone he meets. 7. I have never been to jail, up to now.
Übung 9: 1. My mobile isn't working at the moment. 2. Hudson and Elliot were invited for dinner yesterday. 3. Sir Bernard usually walks very fast. 4. The Montgomerys have a castle in the countryside. 5. Germany has a population of 80 million. 6. Before he moved to London, he lived in Bristol.
Übung 10: 1. a 2. b 3. b 4. b 5. a 6. a
Übung 11: 1. Please send me the order confirmation. 2. Bookkeepers record all purchases. 3. Your cheque is in the mail. 4. Please pay your invoice as soon as possible.
Übung 12: 1. - (Hudson doesn't like tea.) 2. ✔ 3. - (Jeremy Paxton doesn't like anyone.) 4. ✔ 5. - (What does tea-lady mean?) 6. - (Miss Evans has been with the bank for 45 years.)
Übung 13: 1. b 2. c 3. c 4. b
Übung 14: 1. Hudson has interviewed Hugh Montgomery. 2. Somebody has attacked Elvira. 3. Your invoice has been paid. 4. They have found Elvira lying on the floor. 5. I haven't found my mobile phone. 6. Elvira has never had caviar.
Übung 15: 1. end 2. saw 3. helpful 4. talk 5. apprehend 6. face